"Monsieur! Just what are you suggesting?"

That was when Longarm woke up. He opened his eyes and saw that he had Madame Guerard in bed with him. He couldn't move away from her without exposing himself, so instead he said, "Howdy, ma'am. I'm sorry—but, you see, I was having a dirty dream."

She lay beside him. *"Oui,* that seems obvious." Instead of removing his hand from her body she moved it thoughtfully, and he realized she wasn't wearing a petticoat, or anything else, under her skirts...

━◆━ TABOR EVANS ◆━

LONGARM

AND THE FRENCH ACTRESS

A JOVE BOOK

LONGARM AND THE FRENCH ACTRESS

A Jove Book / published by arrangement with
the author

PRINTING HISTORY
Jove edition / May 1983

ISBN: 0-515-06256-1

Jove books are published by Jove Publications, Inc.,
200 Madison Avenue, New York, N.Y. 10016. The words
"A JOVE BOOK" and the "J" with sunburst are trademarks
belonging to Jove Publications, Inc.

PRINTED IN THE UNITED STATES OF AMERICA

Chapter 1

The gent who'd first said virtue was its own reward could not have spent much time west of the Big Muddy. For Disgusting Dan Dillon was sure banking on Longarm behaving sensibly and soberly, and Longarm might have wound up dead if he'd taken the advice of his superior, Marshal Billy Vail, and gone home to bed at a reasonable hour for once.

It was an established fact that federal deputies who hung out in the Black Cat or the Silver Dollar until all hours tended to show up for work the next day late, red-eyed, and unshaven. So when Longarm knocked off at the federal building Tuesday evening, his boss exhorted him to go straight home to his furnished digs and enjoy the experience of a good night's sleep alone for a change.

Longarm said he'd study on it, and he did, as he dined on steak and chili in the one Mexican joint on Larimer Street where they knew how to make chili right. North of Pueblo, cooks tended to get sissy, and you could hardly get enough chili powder in your grub to make your eyes water right. As he started his supper, Longarm was willing to allow that Billy Vail's suggestion made sense. It was a work night, he was running low on pocket money, and he had been overdoing things a mite of late. But by the time he'd washed his steak and chili down with a couple of schooners of needled beer, Longarm was getting his second wind. It was funny how the cool shades of evening woke a man up after a long, tedious day in court. Billy Vail had had him guarding a federal prisoner for the judge and jury all day, and now that they'd decided to hang the son of a bitch, Longarm was aware how many infernal hours he'd spent just sitting. He decided he would sleep better if he walked some of the kinks out of his legs and, since there were only so many directions a man without much cash to jingle could walk in Denver of an evening, Longarm just naturally headed down to Larimer to see if it was still there.

Meanwhile, Disgusting Dan Dillon was laying for Longarm near the Cherry Creek bridge Longarm always crossed, on the way home to his boardinghouse on the less fashionable side of the shallow, sandy wash bisecting Denver's downtown flats. Disgusting Dan was hunkered in literal ambush, his broad back screened by a frame shed someone had once built and then forgot about, his view of the bridge partially obstructed by a weedy tangle of dock and sunflower stalks. The sun was low to the west, so Disgusting Dan knew that to anyone crossing the bridge from the east, he'd be invisible in the shade of the empty shed. He had a buffalo gun across his knees and backed his rifle with a brace of S&W .45s. He was shivering some despite his frock coat and considerable lard. He tried to tell himself he had goose bumps because even in high summer the evenings tended to be cool in Denver. He was too determined, or perhaps too stupid, to allow that he was scared. Disgusting Dan Dillon was not a heavy thinker, even though he weighed three hundred pounds.

Disgusting Dan had led a disgusting life and was fixing to die a disgusting death because he was a creature of his appetites who just never thought ahead far enough to matter. He'd escaped from Yuma Prison less than two weeks before, which wasn't all that dumb when you studied on it. For no man with a lick of sense would have served his time at Yuma had he seen any way of avoiding it.

Disgusting Dan's basic mistake, after getting away clean, was coming to Denver to gun the lawman who'd put him in Yuma in the first place. Sending Disgusting Dan to Yuma hadn't been Longarm's notion. He'd just arrested the fat owlhoot three years before and forgotten about him. The original charge had been stealing Indian beef. Then someone remembered Disgusting Dan's disgusting behavior towards a Pima squaw down along the Gila and, had not he escaped, he'd have likely kept making little rocks out of big ones in the hot Arizona sunshine till he got too old to treat gals so disgusting.

But he had escaped. And, like most of the uncouth gents Longarm dealt with in his line of work, Disgusting Dan seemed to take his arrest as a personal affront. So, as Longarm was entering the Black Cat a mile or more away, Disgusting Dan was starting to get disgusted with waiting.

There wasn't much going on in the Black Cat. But some old pards bought Longarm a beer and told him some dirty jokes to wake him up some more. He marveled, as he headed over to the Silver Dollar, at the springy way his long legs were working, now that he was away from that musty old courtroom. The evening was cool and young. Longarm was starting to feel downright frisky, too. As he strode through the swinging doors of the Silver Dollar, the piano was tinkling a lively jig and the main salon was pleasantly reeking of tobacco smoke and French perfume. The fancy gals who worked at the Silver Dollar didn't stint on their scent. Some of them weren't bad looking, either. But that wasn't why Longarm had come to the Silver Dollar. He was too romantic-natured to pay for the synthetic love of painted pros, no matter what they looked like. He was here to *make* some money, not to pay it out for pleasure.

He spotted the action he was searching for in a far corner. One of the Denver beat coppers, Lord bless him, had told Longarm a new tinhorn was in town. Longarm liked to keep abreast of professional gambling men new to Larimer Street. Not to arrest them—gambling, even crooked gambling, was not a federal offense. Longarm considered tinhorns a legitimate source of extra income. He didn't think it fair to deal from the bottom in a game with honest men. But it only seemed right to take a professional cheater down the garden path, and Longarm was so good at it that none of the local cheats would play with him any more.

The newcomer to Denver was a rat-faced individual wearing a pearl-gray Stetson and a maroon brocaded vest. He was dealing with his back to the corner. Longarm could see why. The tinhorn was shuffling so shamelessly that Longarm could tell he was a mechanic long before he reached the table. Longarm stood politely until a hand he knew from over in the Burlington Yards grinned up at him and asked if he'd like to take his place. Longarm nodded and the hand got up, trying not to laugh. For he knew Longarm of old, but only introduced him as a good old boy he knew from the yards.

The gambler just nodded, hardly looking at Longarm as the tall lawman sat down. The Justice Department made Longarm wear a tobacco-brown suit and shoestring tie on the job, but with his flat-crowned, battered Stetson and old scuffed army boots he likely looked cow enough to the stranger.

The gambler told him chips were a dollar and deuces were wild, if that wasn't too rich for his blood. Longarm said he'd come to play, but added, "If it's all the same to you gents, I'd like to see a fresh deck on the table."

The tinhorn frowned thoughtfully and purred, sort of low, "Where I come from, it's not considered polite to question the dealer's cards, friend."

Longarm nodded pleasantly, but replied. "You're in Denver this evening. Old Tom, the bartender, keeps a drawer full of sealed decks by the cash register and it's considered polite, *here,* to play serious cards with virgin decks."

There was a long, ominous moment of silence as the tinhorn tried to bully Longarm with his slitty eyes. Longarm

4

met his threatening stare with his own innocent gray eyes. The lawman could look friendly as hell when he put his mind to it. "Of course, you're the dealer," he went on. "If you're sort of—uh—*attached* to the deck you brought . . ."

The tinhorn swore softly under his breath, snapped his fingers at a passing waitress in a skirt she should have been ashamed of, and ordered a fresh sealed deck from the bar. Longarm could see how the tinhorn meant to mark the fresh deck with the fancy ring he was wearing on the wrong joint of one finger, but it would take him a spell of dealing. Meanwhile, knowing he'd be playing here at the Silver Dollar sooner or later, Longarm had purchased and pocketed his own set of house cards earlier that week. He'd marked them carefully and unobtrusively to kill time while sitting in that infernal courthouse all afternoon.

So, as the game resumed, Longarm proceeded to steal the tinhorn's money shamelessly. He tried not to cheat the other two gents in the game too much. They were just poor lambs, after all. The tinhorn took some time to catch on. Not having marked the whole deck yet, he ascribed Longarm's winning streak to luck and, knowing how letting a mark win a few big pots early set everyone up for the kill, the tinhorn acted downright cheerful as he accepted his losses—at first. But his joy turned to sadness when, after raking in enough to finance his own modest pleasures until payday, Longarm announced he'd decided to quit while he was ahead.

The tinhorn looked as if he'd been punched in the gut— as well he might have. He'd just about marked the new deck to his liking, or thought he had. He didn't know that Longarm had been switching his own marked cards into the game as it progressed. "Where I come from, it's not considered polite to leave the game so early, friend," he said.

Longarm smiled at him and replied, "This is Denver. Folks are noted, here, for common sense. But I don't want you to think I'm a poor sport. So what say we part friendly by cutting the cards for all I've won against you matching the same?"

The tinhorn's eyes glittered wolfishly as Longarm stood up, reached for the deck uninvited, and shuffled it with one hand as he counted out his winnings on the table. By the time he had the deck face down beside his considerable stack of coins, the tinhorn had come around to his side of the table to match Longarm's bet soberly. The other players moved back. The tinhorn was tense as a coiled sidewinder, and Longarm was taller than anyone else in the place. There was serious money on the table now. The tinhorn purred, dangerously, "High card, deuces wild?"

Longarm nodded. "You called the tune. I'll cut."

"It's still my deal, friend."

There was an ominous silence. In the background a girl murmured, "Oh, dear!" But Longarm just shrugged and told the tinhorn to help his fool self. The tinhorn cut the deck and held up a king with a modest grin. Longarm whistled, reached down, and cut a deuce. It wasn't hard, since he'd shuffled the deck himself. He'd expected the tinhorn to call deuces wild, so he'd crimped all four of them.

Longarm grinned and sort of leaned on the deck with one hand to flatten the cards down decently while he pocketed the pot. The gambling man only had eyes for his vanishing silver dollars. He didn't cotton to what he was seeing, much. "Let's cut again. Double or nothing," he said.

Longarm shook his head with a smile and said, "Another time," as he turned away from the corner table. He wasn't really expecting trouble. Denver was getting mighty civilized these days. But Longarm had played cards in wilder towns in his time. He naturally kept one eye on the mirror over the bar as he headed for the swinging doors. So, even before someone shouted, "Longarm! Duck!" the tall deputy had crabbed sideways and was spinning on one knee, slapping leather, by the time the poor loser had his derringer out of that fancy vest.

Longarm fired first; the tinhorn never fired at all. Longarm's .44 slug took him over the heart and sat him in the corner, on the floor, to bleed his life away with a glassy-eyed stare while Longarm lowered his smoking muzzle to his side.

. . .

Over by the Cherry Creek bridge, Disgusting Dan Dillon
heard the single distant pistol report, but put it down as one
of those things that happened along Larimer Street of an
evening. He wasn't worried about some drunken trail hand
taking umbrage at a streetlight. There were no lights at all
in this seedy neighborhood, and it was getting too dark for
him to make out the far side of the damned bridge. That
was more important than mysterious distant gunshots. Disgusting Dan knew Longarm was too dangerous to open up
on at close range. This ambush had to be reconsidered.
Disgusting Dan didn't believe in giving his victims any
possible break.

The owlhoot who'd told him Longarm came home by
way of the Cherry Creek bridge had told Disgusting Dan
where Longarm roomed as well. But the notion of bearding
Longarm in his own den had sounded about as sensible as
crawling into a beehive, smooth-shaven and naked. But as
the gathering dusk blurred everything within rifle range to
ominous shadows, Disgusting Dan rose from his ambush
and headed for Longarm's boardinghouse to scout it some.

His plan, such as it was, depended on his having a clean
shot at Longarm from a position of invisibility. If there were
a porch lamp burning over the door, a gent across the street
in the shadows had a tolerable chance as Longarm stopped
to let his fool self in. Disgusting Dan Dillon could already
boast half a dozen tolerable guns he'd blowed way. He saw
no need to add that he'd shot all of them in the back or
from cover.

Over at the Silver Dollar, Longarm was feeling mighty
disgusted with himself as he waited for the town law to
arrive. He knew he had to hang about and explain the dead
man in the corner. That didn't worry him. Even the sissy
Denver police allowed that a gent had the right to defend
himself. But Longarm figured to catch pure hell for being
such a fool, once Billy Vail heard he'd been playing cards
in a house of ill repute again. Old President Hayes had been

elected on a reform ticket and folks who worked for the U.S. government these days were supposed to wear neckties and drink sarsaparilla, packing a gun or not.

By now the smoke and the crowd had thinned some. No married man with a lick of sense was about to hang around until the police and reporters for the *Denver Post* arrived. The professor who'd been playing the piano had herded the painted gals out of sight and, upstairs, the madam was pounding on doors to clear the premises. Longarm reloaded and holstered his .44 as he lounged against the bar, talking to the bartender, who was one of the few employees who had to stick around, lest the police take the Silver Dollar for a deserted . . . whatever. The bartender suggested a shot of Maryland rye to steady Longarm while they waited, but Longarm decided to pass this time. He had enough on his plate without being found standing over a dead man with a shotglass in his hand.

Over on the far side of Cherry Creek, Disgusting Dan Dillon had made his way along the cinder paved walks of the dark, deserted, disreputable neighborhood to the boardinghouse his informant had pointed out as Longarm's. Disgusting Dan saw no light upstairs, where Longarm hired his corner room. There was no porch light, but he could see that the landlady had left the gaslight burning in the hallway downstairs. It cast a dim, warm glow through the glass panels of the front door. The old lady who owned the place lived somewhere in the back, he'd heard. She'd likely turned in early, but left the hall light lit, lest one of her boarders wake her tripping over umbrella stands and such when they got home.

The hall light spooked Disgusting Dan out of sneaking up the porch steps to try the door. He knew he'd be outlined to the street by that infernal light if he tried to let himself in. Anyone inside would spot him through the glass, too. But there were many ways to skin a cat. So he crossed the rutted dirt street, keeping to the shadows, and ducked around the corner into the alley behind the boardinghouse.

The moon was rising. The trash cans, board fencing, and

stable doors facing the alley were dark pewter outlined in black ink as he got his bearings. He found the gate to the backyard of the boardinghouse and opened it cautiously. He grinned. The old gal who boarded Longarm kept her hinges greased. So he made not a sound as he let himself into the dark backyard and closed the gate after him.

He stood still long enough to get the lay of the land. The back door had a glass panel, too, so a shaft of gaslight lanced out to spotlight the one-hole outhouse standing tall in the middle of the yard. It reminded Disgusting Dan that he hadn't relieved himself for some time. But gunning Longarm was more important. He eased up on the back porch, looked back over his shoulder, and grinned. His outline was hidden by the bulking blackness of the stable behind the outhouse. On the other hand, he had a clear view down the length of the hall, including the front entrance. He cradled the buffalo gun in his arms and rested his rump on the rail as he settled down to wait, like a big fat cat staked out by a mouse hole. Sooner or later Longarm would be opening that front door. He'd either head for those stairs to the left or come back this way to use the outhouse before turning in. Either way, he was going to catch a .75 buffalo round and considerable busted glass when Disgusting Dan fired through the back door from the darkness.

A couple of uniformed coppers had finally arrived at the Silver Dollar. Since they thought it was all right to have a beer or two while discussing the shootout, Longarm allowed he'd have that Maryland rye after all. The coppers knew Longarm and seemed willing to take his word that the cadaver in the coroner had committed suicide by drawing a derringer against a double-action .44 worn cross-draw by a man as serious-looking as Longarm. But they said they'd have to put Longarm's name in their report, anyway, if only as a witness.

Longarm sighed. "I was afraid you boys would act officious. But, look, if I'm willing to stand up to the coroner and allow I blew the rascal away, could we—uh—make

9

the papers read we shot it out in the street, out front?"

The coppers exchanged uncomfortable glances. They had picky bosses, too. One of them swallowed some beer thoughtfully and sighed. "I feel for you, Longarm. But I just can't reach you. You know we ain't allowed to move the body till the coroner's meat wagon gets here. The coroner's man is duty bound to record when and where he picked the stiff up. And how would it look if the coroner's jury had reports conflicting total?"

His partner suggested, "What if you was to say you spotted the rascal out on the street and chased him in here to arrest him, Longarm? That way nobody could say you was in the Silver Dollar as a customer—right?"

Longarm shook his head. "Too many folks saw me playing cards with the bastard for me to get away with such a whopper. Besides, I'd be sore pressed to show how a federal deputy had call to arrest a tinhorn gambling man. What he was doing with his private deck was shameful, but I doubt it was a federal offense."

A stubby man in a derby and checked suit came in, waving a pad of yellow paper in one hand and a pencil stub in the other. "I just heard Longarm has another notch in his gun," he said. "Who was it this time, and how do I report it to our readership?"

"Simmer down, Crawford," Longarm said. "We ain't figured out the story yet." He nodded at the bartender. "Old Crawford and the *Post* are drinking with me, as long as he keeps still and gives me time to sort this mess out."

The reporter bellied up to the bar and said he'd have a beer and a shot. But then he spread his notebook on the mahogany and Longarm could see that he was already writing things down. Crawford asked what the dead man's name was. It seemed like a sensible question. One of the coppers stepped over to the still-seated corpse in the corner and knelt to go through his pockets.

Longarm told Crawford, "If you tell fibs about me *this* time, Crawford, we ain't going to be pards no more, hear?"

"I'm just doing my job, damn it!" Crawford protested.

"What's a reporter supposed to do when a notorious gunslick like you shoots a tourist in a whorehouse—report it as a social event?"

The copper who'd checked out the cadaver rejoined them, holding a pigskin wallet open. "According to this, the gent you shot was one William R. Murgatroid. There ain't no calling cards, but it's stamped on the leather in gold."

Longarm blinked in surprise and held out his hand. "Let me see that!"

The copper handed it over. "Murgatroid sure is a funny name," he commented.

The reporter wrote it down, but said, "He might have made it up." Then he saw that Longarm was grinning like a sly old fox in a henhouse. So, being a good reporter, Crawford asked, "What am I missing, Longarm?"

"My reprieve," Longarm said. "You're right about Murgatroid being a sort of unusual name," he told the policeman. "That's how come I remember it."

"You mean William R. Murgatroid was wanted by the law?"

"Not hardly. William R. Murgatroid was a mining man up Leadville way. He got shot in the back room of a saloon in Leadville last spring, by a person or persons unknown. They found him on the floor surrounded by scattered playing cards. It wasn't federal, but I read the flier sent out by the Lake County sheriff."

He nodded at the dead tinhorn in the corner. "Put it together, boys. The late William R. Murgatroid was relieved of his cash and this fancy, expensive pigskin wallet by someone he was playing cards with alone up Leadville way. The gent over there with my round in him fancied pretty duds and gear. He should have throwed this wallet away after, but anyone can see it's a mighty handsome one— and, what the hell, he figured he'd got clean away with no witnesses to the shootout he won."

One of the coppers snapped his fingers. "Hot damn! He was new in Denver, too. I can see it all now. After gunning that mining man and lifting his wad, he laid low for a spell, and then rode into our fair city to resume his wild and wicked ways."

His partner started to elaborate, but the reporter said, "I know how the rest goes, damn it. Let me put it down. Old Longarm, here, spotted the dead man's wallet and followed the gambler in here to get the goods on him. Only the murderer suspicioned Longarm was on to him and went for his gun. Ain't that about the way it went, Longarm?"

Longarm resisted an impulse to jingle the silver dollars in his pocket as he nodded modestly. "That's close enough," he said.

So they had a drink on it and, by the time the horse-drawn ambulance arrived to clean up the mess, Crawford had left to file his story and Longarm was feeling a lot better.

The night was still young for Longarm, and he now had the wherewithal for some hooting and hollering indeed. But, after signing his statement, he decided to be sensible for a change and go on home. He was out of the woods as far as the newspapers were concerned, but there were some awesome holes in his story and he knew that Marshal Vail would expect him to show up bright and early with sensible answers. So he headed home to his furnished digs to establish the fact he was a working man of sober habits. Billy Vail was sure to check.

Like most men who spent time in the saddle, Longarm wore boots. But since a lawman spent more time on his feet than a cowhand, he walked spurless and low-heeled in surplus cavalry stovepipes. So he made good time getting home. Having long legs and being sober helped.

He clunked a mite, crossing the Cherry Creek bridge, but despite his size and stride, Longarm walked almost as silently as an Indian. As he spied the hall light of his rooming house ahead, he slowed and walked even more quietly. He wasn't out to sneak up on his landlady; he just didn't want to wake her up. The poor old gal was still angry with him for busting the bed upstairs with that Mexican gal one night. He knew if she heard him coming in she'd pop out of bed

12

and peek out at him, and he never knew what to say to a lady in a nightgown when he wasn't figuring to leap into bed with her.

The beers he'd consumed earlier were working through Longarm's kidneys now. And, unbeknownst to him, Disgusting Dan Dillon's mind had been running in the same channels. He'd about given up on his intended victim ever getting home. It was late as hell, they said Longarm had an eye for the ladies, and how long could anyone hang about on a back porch dying to squat and drop it?

So, as Longarm approached the front of the boarding-house, Disgusting Dan eased down the back steps and tip-toed over to the outhouse. He found those hinges were silent, too, and sighed with satisfaction as he shut the door, leaned the buffalo gun in a corner, and dropped his britches to settle his considerable bare ass on the one hole. He relieved his bowels with a pig-like sigh, found a mail-order catalogue nailed to one wall, tore off a sheet, and wiped himself. Then he rose, buckled up, and was about to open the door when he heard someone else opening a door somewhere in the night.

Disgusting Dan snatched up his buffalo gun, dry-mouthed with sudden fear as he tried to peer out the half-moon cutout in the otherwise solid plank door. He was too short, so he climbed up on the seat, with a boot braced on either side of the hole. Now the infernal half-moon was too *low!* But, by shoving the stubby barrel of the rifle through the cutout to brace himself, he could lean forward to peer out, teetering on the seat planks at an awkward angle.

It didn't do Disgusting Dan much good. As Longarm came out the back door he was looking straight at the out-house door, that being his intended destination, when he saw the moon- and lamp-lit muzzle of a considerable gun poking out of the half-moon cutout at him.

What followed thereafter was what anyone but an owl-hoot as dumb as Disgusting Dan might have foreseen before going after a gunslick like Longarm in the first place. Long-arm crabbed sideways out of the light as he drew and fired

13

four shots right through the craphouse door. He rolled over the porch rail to land in a crouch in the foundation plantings to reload as he listened to the awesome results of his first fusilade.

Disgusting Dan Dillon's death was almost as disgusting as the life he'd led. When Longarm's four rounds and a mess of pine splinters slashed into his lard-bucket gut, the fat man slammed back against the rear wall and slid down it to land sitting on the thin plank seat. Since it had never been designed to stand up to such falling weight, Disgusting Dan just kept going.

He landed, gunshot and screaming, in four feet of lime-dusted, semi-liquid shit. The lime folks dropped atop their leavings had formed a slight crust that normally kept the stink within reason, but as the criminal wallowed like a walrus in the bottom of the pit, the stench rose to the heavens.

By this time windows all around were flying open and everyone was yelling a lot. Longarm's landlady came to the back door, wrapped in a dressing gown and wailing like a banshee. Longarm, having reloaded and guessed what was going on over there, told her to get back inside while he checked out the condition of her sanitary facilities.

He moved in at an angle, gun leveled, and simply kicked the outhouse over, exposing the pit and its contents to view. The view was almost as disgusting as the stench. He started to strike a match, then remembered the gases might be explosive and settled for staring down by moonlight. What looked like a big pile of shit down there was groaning and pleading, "Help me, damnit! Give me your hand!"

"Not hardly," Longarm said. "How bad are you hit—and who the hell are you?"

"I'm gutshot, you son of a bitch! Get me out of here! I needs me a doc, quick!"

"We'll study on that after you tell me who you are and how come you were laying for me in such a disgusting place."

The man in the pit didn't answer. He couldn't. His head

14

had gone under, and after a time the ghastly bubbling stopped. Longarm drew his gun again, figuring a few more shots at the moon ought to bring some coppers. But then he heard a whistle and running footsteps, so he put his gun away.

Longarm knew the beat copper who joined him by the overturned outhouse. The copper knew Longarm, too. "I figured the shots came from somewhere close to you, Longarm," he said. "That Colt Model T of yours is getting to be a familiar sound on my beat, cuss your hide! Who'd you shoot this time?"

Longarm said, "Beats the shit out of me." He chuckled dryly. "Come to think of it, the coroner's boys will have to *clean* the shit off of him before anyone can figure out who the hell he might have been."

He filled the copper in. There wasn't all that much to tell. The copper had heard about the earlier shootout in the Silver Dollar. "Do you reckon the gent down there was a sidekick of the tinhorn you had it out with earlier, Longarm?" he asked.

Longarm shrugged. "Don't know. I don't even want to look at his infernal face, till someone hoses him down."

Chapter 2

Longarm knew he was in for it as soon as he got to the office in the federal building the next morning. Henry, the prissy clerk who played the typewriter out front, had a copy of the morning extra on his desk and a teacher's-pet expression on his pimpled face as he said, "Go right in. Marshal Vail has been waiting for you, Deputy Long."

Longarm lit a cheroot and let himself into the inner sanctum to face the music and Billy Vail. Longarm could see by the banjo clock on the oak-paneled wall that he was two minutes early for a change. Nobody but sissies got to work any earlier than that, even when they had a boss like Billy Vail.

Chief Marshal Billy Vail was shorter, older, and fatter than Longarm. But as he glared at his deputy from behind his mahogany desk, he still looked mean as hell. "Damn it, Longarm, it ain't safe to let you roam the streets of Denver without a leash!" he said. "What in thunder got into you last night? This is Denver, the capital of Colorado and the metropolis of the Rocky Mountain empire, not Dodge City!"

Longarm sat down in the leather guest chair across the desk from Vail. "Don't get your bowels in an uproar, boss," he said soothingly. "You can see I got me a necktie on this morning, can't you?"

"Yeah, and I've been meaning to talk to you about the bullet holes in that old Stetson, too. But I'm not talking about how sloppy you dress, old son. According to this morning's *Post,* you killed two men last night within two hours. Is that any way for a federal employee to act, damn it? We're working for a reform administration, Longarm. The voters elected President Hayes because they were tired of the shoot-'em-up cowboy days of U. S. Grant and the Indian Ring."

Longarm blew a thoughtful smoke ring and replied, "I got sort of tired of cleaning up after them crooks, too. Old Grant left the West in a mess it ain't recovered from yet. But what I done last night was pure as the driven snow, Billy. I know you expect me to shave and look pretty these days, but I'm still supposed to go after outlaws, and the two I tangled with last night add up to two wanted murderers. A murderer and a half, leastways. We finally figured out the one I shot in the outhouse was Disgusting Dan Dillon, wanted for all sorts of disgusting deeds, including the killing of a guard as he was saying *adios* to Yuma Prison a few days ago. The other one is still up for grabs. We figure he killed the gent whose wallet he was packing, but we still don't know who he was."

Billy Vail shook his head like a bull with a fly between its horns and snapped, "Never mind whether you should or should not have shot 'em. The point is that you shot one in a whorehouse and one in a shithouse! Have you any notion what a poor impression that makes on the folks who read the *Post,* Longarm?"

Longarm chuckled. "It is sort of humorous, the way old Crawford wrote it up. But what would you have done in my place, Billy? Both those boys had drawn on me before I fired one shot at either!"

Vail suppressed a smile as he lowered his eyes to the papers piled like autumn leaves on his green blotter. "I've granted an interview to some other reporters this afternoon," he said. "I want you out of sight and out of mind when it occurs. I can put things delicate to newspaper men. I don't

18

want you telling any more reporters that you can't claim Dillon for your guns since the coroner's report says he drowned."

Vail found the letter he was looking for and nodded as he scanned it again. "I'm sending you north to Cheyenne to meet a train that's due in this afternoon. It's a delicate job, and God knows you ain't delicate, but we've been requested to send somebody, and I want you out of my hair for a spell."

Longarm was too polite to comment on the little hair Vail had left on his pink bullet head. He blew another smoke ring and said, "I'm on my way, as soon as Henry types up my travel vouchers and such. What about this mysterious train, boss? Is somebody out to rob it, or is there a suspect aboard you want arrested?"

"Neither," Vail said. "I just said it was delicate. Lord give me strength. I sure wish I had someone more civilized to send, but my other deputies are as bad as you and some of 'em ain't as smart."

"Thanks—I think. Are you aiming to tell me what's so delicate up there, or do I just have to guess?"

"Have you ever heard of Sarah Bernhardt?"

"The French actress? Sure I have. I ain't ignorant. I read the *Police Gazette* regular, and they had a picture of her in tights a spell back. She ain't built bad. They call her the Divine Sarah. But why are we jawing about the Divine Sarah, Billy? She lives in Paris, France, the last I heard."

"The Divine Sarah and her troupe are touring the U. S. in a special theater train. It's due to arrive in Cheyenne this afternoon. This evening, Miss Sarah is putting on a performance of *King Lear* at the Cheyenne Civic Auditorium. I ain't sure if she's playing King Lear or one of his daughters. But you can wire me about it after you get there."

Longarm studied the tip of his cheroot as he mused, "It won't work neither way, Billy. Miss Sarah studies to be about thirty-five right now. So she's too young to play King Lear and a mite long in the tooth to be one of his teenage daughters. Come to think on it, she's about right for *me,*

19

though. Like I said, I've seen her picture in tights."

Vail looked stricken. "Longarm, so help me God, if you wind up in bed with the national treasure of France, I'll feed your heart to the hawks! That's an *order,* Longarm! You're not to trifle with the Divine Sarah, even if invited! Do I have your word on that? I really *mean* it this time!"

"Just funning," Longarm chuckled. "I don't savvy enough French to matter, anyways. But if you don't want me flirting with old Sarah, what in thunder are you sending me up there to do? I don't fancy a life upon the wicked stage, even if I knew how to act."

"She's got actors," Vail said. "A whole trainload of 'em. She had Secret Service bodyguards as far west as Omaha. But the First Lady found out about it, and now President Hayes has a choice of sleeping on the sofa or causing an international incident with France. You see, our State Department told the Frog ambassador that the Secret Service would naturally guard the Divine Sarah's fair white body from Injuns and such whilst she was touring the States for the first time. But then Lemonade Lucy Hayes found out about it, and she had a terrible fit!"

Longarm frowned and asked, "What's the First Lady got against Sarah Bernhardt, Billy? It ain't like they travel in the same circles—and I doubt old Lemonade Lucy reads the *Police Gazette.*"

"The president's wife must have read something somewhere. It's no secret that the Divine Sarah is—well—French. Worse yet, she drinks wine in public. You know, of course, that the First Lady is honorary head of the Women's Christian Temperance Union, so . . ."

"I see the light," Longarm said with a laugh. Then he sobered some as he added reflectively, "Whether Miss Sarah Bernhardt meets with the approval of the W.C.T.U. or not don't get around the fact that the U.S. government told the French government we'd look after her. I didn't know the First Lady got to boss the Secret Service around!"

"She doesn't—officially. On the other hand, a married man has problems, even when he's President of these United

States. As I understand it, the First Lady was satisfied to learn that the gents who guard her and the White House won't be guarding what she considers a soiled dove. Meanwhile, since the French don't know a Secret Service agent from a Justice Department deputy, the job's been slipped to *us,* sort of under the table."

Longarm shrugged. "Well, I'll head north and see if I can keep the Sioux and such from hissing at tonight's performance. But are those all the orders you have for me, Billy?"

"Sure. What other orders do you need? I know it's a fool's errand, but you're a fool, so it's fitting. Before turning the case over to us, the Secret Service looked into any possible plots against the Divine Sarah. It ain't like she's a political figure the anarchists would be likely to toss a bomb at. I can detail some extra deputies to you if you like, but it's just a routine case of general bodyguarding."

Longarm stood up, saying, "I got the picture, and I like to work solo, anyway. Uncle Sam just wants somebody representing him in the unlikely case them actors run into the usual greenhorn tourist troubles—right?"

Marshal Vail agreed that that was about the size of it. So Longarm went to get a shave and a haircut while Henry arranged his run up to Cheyenne on the noonday Burlington.

In another part of Denver, two hard-eyed men had already bought their tickets to Cheyenne and were staying out of sight until the Burlington Flier was ready to board. One sat by the window with his pistol in his lap, watching the street through the curtains, as his comrade prepared the infernal device they intended to plant under the stage of the Cheyenne Civic Auditorium before that evening's performance. It was timed to go off in the middle of the second act— when the Divine Sarah would be center stage.

The trouble with railroads was that they ran on timetables as well as tracks. So Longarm had some time to kill before the Burlington Flier left, even after he'd gotten prissed up

21

to meet the Divine Sarah in Cheyenne. He had often wished for some form of transportation with the freedom of walking or riding combined with the speed of a steam locomotive. But it hardly seemed likely they'd invent such a critter in his lifetime. So he field-stripped, cleaned, and reloaded his Winchester, derringer, and Colt; picked up a French phrase book; and still had time for a couple of beers before he ambled over to the Union Depot to see if the infernal Flier was set up to go.

It was, but they weren't boarding her yet. In the waiting room, Longarm ran into Crawford of the *Post,* jawing with a handsome ash-blonde lady with an impossible hat and waistline. The hat was impossible because it had ripe cherries sprouting out of it way too late in the year for spring pickings. Her waistline was impossible because human women just weren't built like that. The gal was young and pretty, but running past pleasantly plump into a weight problem she'd best start studying on by the time she was thirty. She had the bare beginnings of a double chin under her heart-shaped face, and her chest stuck out like a pouter pigeon's. Her rump wasn't all that tiny either, but she'd somehow cinched her waist to around eighteen inches. Longarm was damned if he could see how the poor little thing could breathe. Since he was on friendly terms with the reporter, it seemed only neighborly to join them. He was too polite to warn her that she figured to cut herself in two with her corset as Crawford introduced them.

The gal was named Penelope Wayne, but her friends called her Penny. Crawford explained that Miss Penny was an actress and that she was headed up to Cheyenne to ask Sarah Bernhardt for a job. When the plump blonde found out that Longarm was going to bodyguard the Divine Sarah, she started batting her lashes at him even harder. This took some effort, as she'd already started sending signals with her china blue eyes before discovering Longarm was connected with the theater. That was what she called play-acting.

"We'll have to talk about it on the train, Mr. Long," she

22

said. "I'd be pleased to read for you. I have just oodles of scripts in my carpetbag."

Longarm had noticed the big old bag at her feet and was already resigned to carrying it for her once they called "All aboard!" He had his own possibles in a smaller bag, so if he tucked the Winchester in its case under one arm it figured to balance out.

Crawford was looking at him, amused, so Longarm said, "I reckon you have my colors made out wrong, Miss Penny. I'd be pleased as punch to watch you play-act, but I ain't connected with the show in any way. Like I said, I'm only headed north to bodyguard a guest of the U.S. government."

The blonde nodded, but insisted brightly, "That still means you will know Sarah Bernhardt, Custis. I'd do most *anything* to get a proper introduction to her!"

Longarm frowned down at her thoughtfully. "Hold on. I thought you already knew the Divine Sarah. Are you saying you're riding the Flier all the way to Cheyenne just on the chance she'll talk to you?"

Before the would-be actress could answer, a distant voice called, "Next stop, Cheyenne! All a-boooard!"

Penny headed out to the platform without waiting to see if Longarm picked up her big bag or not. He did, of course, as Crawford laughed and said, "Good hunting, Longarm. I sure wish *I* was tall and pretty!"

Longarm grimaced as he grumped out after the blonde, cursing under his breath. Both the gal and that fool reporter sure were taking a lot for granted. He had no intention of getting mixed up with a stagestruck sass, good-looking or not. The Flier would carry them both to Cheyenne—Lord willing and it didn't jump the tracks—long before he could get anywhere with her. Once they were in Cheyenne and he was riding herd on a whole trainload of French actresses, what in thunder would he want with Penelope Wayne?

He caught up with her as she was boarding one of the forward Pullman cars. The porter relieved Longarm of their gear. As he helped the blonde up the steps he noticed she had trouble making them. Between the tight cinch around her middle and the thin air of Denver, Penny was gasping like a fish out of water by the time Longarm had her aboard, even though he was carrying some of her not inconsiderable weight.

"Are you all right?" he asked.

"Yes," she wheezed. "I just had one of my dizzies for a moment there. I've always been rather delicate. But I'm all right now. My compartment's down this way, I think."

That seemed likely, as the porter was toting all their earthly belongings along the corridor. But, as the porter opened a door and ducked in, Longarm asked, "Why did you hire a compartment, Miss Penny? The Burlington Flier doesn't really fly, of course, but it does get to Cheyenne pretty fast, even slowing down for cows on the track in some places."

"I always travel first class," she said, as she entered her compartment.

The porter placed their possibles on one of the seats facing each other in the little cubbyhole. Longarm tipped him a dime and the man discreetly shut the door after him, leaving them alone together.

Penny was already seated, flushed and gasping again as she fanned her face with the hat she'd removed. Longarm took his own hat off and tossed it onto the luggage across the way as he sat beside her. There was no place else to sit. He knew that at night the seats could be folded together into a bunk, and that what looked like a dry sink in the corner lifted up to reveal a private commode. He didn't have to go. On the other hand, he knew that his own hired seat was back in the coaches and the gal was uncomfortable, dressed so proper.

"This compartment's on the shady side," he said. "It'll be cooler in here once the train starts up. But, if I were you, I'd study on—uh—loosening your duds a mite in private."

"Loosening my *what?* Whatever are you suggesting, Custis?"

24

"I ain't suggesting it for *me*, Miss Penny. I'll be riding back in the coaches and you'll be locked in private behind a solid door. It's likely to get hotter before it gets cooler this afternoon, and you'll sure arrive more comfortable if you—well—unlace yourself a mite."

The train began to roll. Penny laughed archly and said, "I do believe you're mentioning my unmentionables, Custis! Are you always so forward with girls you have at your mercy?"

He said, "I ain't being forward, and you ain't at anyone's mercy, Miss Penny. I know it ain't right to mention a lady's unmentionables, but yours are about to strangle you to death. And it's my job to prevent the death of innocent, law-abiding citizens whenever possible. We're a mile above sea level, and you ain't giving your innards enough room to breathe at *any* altitude. I know it's fashionable for gals to look like wasps this season. But, after I leave, you'd best study on letting yourself out a notch or two, hear?"

Before she could answer, the conductor rapped on the door and stepped in to punch their tickets. The conductor knew Longarm of old, so he didn't ask what he was doing in a compartment with a coach ticket. As the conductor left, smiling smugly, Longarm started to get up, too.

"Would you mind opening the window, Custis?" Penny asked. "It's terribly stuffy in here."

Longarm shook his head. "They're burning soft coal up ahead, and the wind is off the Front Range. You'll get soot and fly ash all over you."

"But it's getting hotter. I can't stand it!"

"Aw, come on, it ain't *that* hot in here, Miss Penny. You're just het up and flusterpated by the excitement of the trip, and that fool cinch around your gut. If I was to leave you here with the window open and your face sweated up like that, you'd be auditioning for a part in a minstrel show instead of Shakespeare, if and when you meet the Divine Sarah in Cheyenne this evening."

He got to his feet and reached for his things, adding. "Lock the door after me and peel down some. Everybody

riding first class does. That's why rich folks arrive everywhere looking so calm and snooty."

She rose, too, saying something about reading for him.
Then her eyes went glassy and she started to fall forward
like a tree chopped off just above the roots. She would have
landed on her face had Longarm not dropped his gear in
time to catch her.

He cursed her limp dead weight as he carried her over
to the seat they'd just left and laid her lengthwise, head
down and feet up on the armrest. When that didn't work,
he stepped over to the corner sink above the hidden commode and ran water over his pocket handkerchief until it
felt cool. He returned to Penny's side, knelt, and dabbed
her flushed face. She moaned and tried to take a deep breath.
That didn't work either.

Longarm shrugged, put the damp cloth aside, and rolled
her over on to her stomach to unbutton her tight bodice
down the back. He didn't mean to undress her completely.
That wouldn't have been decent. But after he had her dress
open he found that the infernal corset was under a silk
chemise. So he had to haul that up until her bare back and
behind bulged naked on either side of the impossibly tight
corset. He was a mite surprised to discover that she wore
no underdrawers. But, what the hell, she was lying face
down.

Longarm went to work on the laces of her corset. He
could see that most of the problem lay in the torture device
being way the hell too small and narrow for a girl of Penny's
size. Her innards might have accommodated themselves to
the eighteen-inch waist she fancied if the constriction had
been spread out more reasonably. But, as he'd suspected,
she wore a narrow band no wider than a Mexican's sash,
damned near cutting her in two. As he loosened the laces,
her waist ballooned out to a sensible mid-section for a gal
built so heroic. She still was shaped sort of like an hourglass—even more so, now that he could gaze down at her
naked spine from the tailbone up. But he averted his gaze
politely as he tossed the corset aside and proceeded to button
her dress again.

The relieved blonde raised her head from the green plush. "What am I doing in this position? Oh, dear—are you undressing me?"

He said, "No, ma'am. I'm buttoning the other way. How does it feel to breathe again?"

"Heavenly. But I suddenly feel so strange. Have you been . . . trifling with me?"

"I just allowed I hadn't. Just lay still and I'll let myself out."

But she grabbed his hand and held it as she swung herself into a sitting position, saying, "Wait! Don't go. I'm still confused."

He sat down beside her again and she looked at him oddly, ran a hand over her mid-section, and marveled, "My corset's gone! You *did* undress me!"

"Not enough to matter. Your cinch strap's yonder, by your hat, Miss Penny. Take my advice and get rid of it. You don't really need the fool thing, and it seems to be the cause of your dizzy spells."

She sucked in her gut, thoughtfully and asked, "Don't you find me a little too plump, Custis?"

"You could lose twenty pounds without drying up and blowing away, ma'am. But you're still a handsome woman, and trying to look skinny by strangling your natural charms is just dumb."

"I have to do *something* for my figure. I'm embarrassed by my actual measurements. You'd never guess what I really am around the waist."

Longarm thought that was silly, since he'd just seen her naked from the tailbone north. But he smiled gallantly and lied, "I'm a fair judge of woman-flesh, Miss Penny. So I don't reckon I'd be far off if I guessed twenty-four inches, without the fool cinch."

It pleased her, as he had known it would. "That's close enough," she smiled. "But I still mean to put my corset back on before we get to Cheyenne—and you're going to have to help me with it."

He frowned. "Are you sure your family would approve of this line of talk, ma'am?"

"Silly! There's nobody here but us to approve or disapprove. Besides, I know I can trust you now. You had your chance to take advantage of me when you took my corset off. So why should you act fresh when you help me put it back on?"

He didn't answer. It was too dumb a question. Naturally, no gent who had to face himself shaving in the morning was about to climb aboard any unconscious she-male. But being invited to fiddle with the unmentionables of a wide-awake and flirty-eyed blonde was another temptation entirely.

The train had picked up speed and the roof vents were starting to work better now, but it was still a mite stuffy in the compartment. So, as long as she seemed to want him to stay, Longarm asked if it was all right with her if he took off his coat and vest. Penny said it was, and added that his suggestion about informal wear while traveling privately made a lot of sense. "If I took off my dress and put it away, we could have the window open a crack, couldn't we? I mean, it hardly matters if I get my chemise a little sooty, and we could wash up before we reached Cheyenne."

He started to object. Then he told himself not to be a fool. He wasn't the one who'd started sending smoldering signals with his big blue eyes. The gal was over twenty-one, and it was her compartment.

So, as Penny rose to make room, Longarm slid over to the window and put his back into opening it a crack despite the best efforts of paint and grime to discourage the notion. It did feel grand when a cool gust of dry prairie air lanced in at them. He figured it was even safe to smoke now. As he leaned back, fishing in his shirt pocket for a cheroot, he saw that Penny had stripped down to her thin silk chemise, and she surely filled it out well. He already knew that she wore no drawers above her black silk stockings and high-button shoes.

As she sat down beside him again he saw that she wore nothing across her big, firm breasts. Her nipples were turgid under the thin silk. He hadn't planned it, but he was feeling

28

sort of turgid himself, though not across his chest. He decided to skip the smoke. His mouth was watering, but it wasn't for tobacco.

Now that she had started breathing right, Penny's smooth complexion had taken on a healthy peaches-and-cream glow. There was a lot of complexion to see, since the chemise was cut low. Her shoulders were nicely shaped and her pleasantly plump bare arms looked as though they'd hug well.

A little black fleck of fly ash settled on her left cheek. Longarm laughed and smudged it off with his thumb to be polite.

She must not have known what he was doing, for she pressed his hand to her cheek with both her hands, moved her lips into his palm, and kissed it, licking it with her pointy pink tongue for good measure. He blinked in surprise, then grinned and reeled her in to kiss her right, and damned if she didn't use her tongue that way, too.

He lowered her into a more sensible position as she pulled her chemise up out of the way to let him explore her with his free hand. There wasn't anything between her collarbone and her garters he'd never felt before, of course, but the nice thing about women was that no matter how many he explored, they all felt swell. He got his hand between her plump creamy thighs and proceeded to warm them both up some more before getting to the tactically dangerous part, where he had to let go long enough to shuck his own duds. She was built between the legs like gals were supposed to be, and she responded to his skilled fingers by kissing harder and rotating her ample hips. His fingers told him that Penny was built tight for such a big gal, and since she was nicely lubricated, now, and not objecting as he kept on kissing her, Longarm gave up his advantage for the moment and started unbuttoning and unbuckling more fool duds than he remembered putting on that morning.

He was fair shucked when the blonde rolled her lips from his for air and moaned, "Oh, you don't know what you're doing to me, Custis."

29

He was too polite to tell her how silly that sounded. Gals always said dumb things at the last moment. He put his hand back between her thighs and started to mount her, but she crossed her legs and protested. "Wait! We have to settle a few things first."

He stopped in mid-stroke. "Oh? I hope you ain't discussing a business transaction, Penny. For, if you are a businesswoman, this sure is a hell of a time to let me in on it."

"Don't be beastly! I'm an actress, not a whore!"

"That's what I thought. I sure wish you'd unlock them knees, honey."

"I will. I want to. But you have to promise me something in return."

"If you don't want money, what in thunder *do* you want?"

"You have to introduce me to Sarah Bernhardt when we get to Cheyenne."

Longarm sighed, raised some of his weight off her, and said, "I'm sure sorry we started this nonsense, ma'am. It was my fault. I should have known better. But, what the hell, no harm's done. We can still part friendly, soon as I figure out where that one boot went."

As he released her and rose to his knees, staring wistfully down at her naked curves, Penny looked astonished and gasped, "What are you talking about? Don't you . . . *want* me?"

"Sure I do. If you'll lower your maidenly gaze, you'll see that you still have my undivided attention. But I wanted you as a man wants a woman, Penny. I'm just a horny old hand, not an infernal theatrical agent."

"But, Custis, you know Sarah Bernhardt!"

"No, I don't. Never seen the lady yet. That's why this ain't going to work, Penny. Don't try to understand me. Sometimes I don't understand me, either. But I reckon I'm just a romantic fool. For it surely cools me off a heap when even a gal as handsome as you starts adding conditions to her surrender."

Penny started to cry. Longarm sat with his bare hip against

hers and patted her shoulder fondly. "Look, when we get to Cheyenne and I meet up with the Divine Sarah, I'll ask her if she's hiring. I'd do that for anyone. But now we'd best get dressed and say no more about it."

"You're crazy!" she sobbed. "That's all I asked you to do in the first place!"

"I know. I told you not to try to understand it, Penny. Oh, there's my boot—yonder under the other seat."

But, as he leaned away from her, Penny grabbed his hand and pressed it to her breast, pleading, "Please don't go! Please don't be angry with me!"

"I ain't angry. Disappointed, maybe. You see, I thought you'd want me for my own self. I never figured you were stagestruck enough to do this just for an introduction. You must have taken me for a horny fool. I can't say I blame you, for I am. But don't cry any more, Penny. I told you I wasn't sore at you."

She sat up, pressing her breast against his side as she reached into his lap, grabbed, and hung on. "I don't care what happens when we get to Cheyenne. I want this *in* me, *now!*"

Longarm started to shake his head, but Penny was shaking something else, and the more she shook it, the less sensible leaving struck him. So, having laid all his cards on the table, Longarm sighed and proceeded to lay Penny Wayne on the green plush seat. As she wrapped her soft arms and legs around him and started rolling under him in time to his thrusts, Longarm wondered what they'd been fussing about just now. They sure seemed totally in agreement when it came to the most enjoyable way to ride to Cheyenne together.

Chapter 3

By the time the Burlington Flier pulled into Cheyenne, Longarm and Penny were good pals. Although they were a mite saddle sore, there were still a few positions they hadn't gotten around to yet. So Longarm checked himself and Penny into the hotel across from the depot as man and wife. The room clerk knew better—Longarm had stayed there before—but it looked more decent that way on the hotel register.

Penny had learned her lesson and hadn't mentioned Longarm's furthering her stage career again, so he had decided to do what he could for her. Penny's rump was tender from rollicking bare on the prickly green plush aboard the Flier. Longarm told her to take a long, hot soak in the adjoining bath while he found out if the Divine Sarah's train had arrived. He knew he'd want a bath himself before he climbed between those slick linen sheets with Penny later. But business came before pleasure, and he'd promised Billy Vail that he'd wire him as soon as he met up with the French touring company.

As he headed for the rail yards, packing only his derringer and sidearm, he spied two long shadows overtaking his own from either side. He stopped and turned. The two hard-eyed gents who'd been trying to fall in on either side with the afternoon sun so low stopped, too. Longarm nodded at them and asked, "Do I know you gents?"

"No, but we know you, Longarm," said one of them. "We know why you came to Cheyenne, and our boss don't like it much!"

Longarm smiled thinly and replied, "Since you know all about me. I'd like to hear more about you. I've already asked once, polite."

The one who hadn't spoken before looked warily down at Longarm's gun hand and hastily said, "Hold on—we're U.S. deputies, too!"

Longarm laughed with relief. "I'm sure glad to hear that," he said, "since it was shaping up two to one, with the sun at your backs. But what beef could the Cheyenne federal marshal have with me and mine, boys? I only came up here to meet some French folks and make sure they don't get lost, scalped, or overcharged."

"That's what we just heard," said the taller of the two. "How come the Denver office got the job? Does Washington think we're too crude-natured to meet the Divine Sarah?"

"You both look as civilized as me—no offense," Longarm said. "But you boys have a burr under your tails over nothing. They never sent me up to guard the Divine Sarah around Cheyenne. Everyone knows them French actors are safe here on *your* beat. The job I'm stuck with is joining up with them and guarding them once they *leave* Cheyenne, see? I'm only meeting 'em here because—hell, I had to meet 'em *someplace*. As I understand it, the Divine Sarah's only giving one performance here in Cheyenne. After that, her and her troupe's headed west over the South Pass into country infested with Shoshone, Mormons, and such. They should have told your office about it. I can see you're justified in feeling left out."

The other deputies exchanged glances. Then the taller one stuck out his hand and said, "I'm Tom McArtle and this here's Phil Woods. Now that we sees you're a sensible gent, we'll tell the boss he went off a mite half-cocked. Is there anything we can do to back your play, Longarm?"

There wasn't, but as Longarm shook his head he detected a certain wistfulness. "That'd be neighborly, Tom," he said. "As you can see, I'm only one man, and I ain't too sure what I'm getting into. If your office can spare you, I'd sure like to have you backing me while the outfit's here in Cheyenne. The first thing I have to do is find out when Miss Bernhardt's train gets in."

"We already know," Woods said. "It's due in about an hour."

Longarm nodded. "There you go. You've helped me already, and I mean to put your names in the night letter I'll be sending later."

He saw that that set well with them. He already knew where the Civic Auditorium was, but he asked them anyway, and they told him what he already knew. "Well, there's nothing for any of us to do until they get here," he said. "What say we all meet later at the auditorium?"

McArtle asked eagerly, "Will we get to meet the famous French gal, Longarm?"

"Hell, you'll have to!" Longarm said. "I'm counting on you boys to help me tonight during the play."

"Doing what?"

"Security. Secret Service suspicions someone may try and spoil the Divine Sarah's first American tour by messing up her performances. Since you boys are based here in Cheyenne, you'd know better than me if anyone in the audience was a suspicious character, right?"

Woods said, "Hot damn! I follows your drift, Longarm. There ain't a troublemaker in town I can't spot at rifle range. But are you saying me and Tom here will get to see the show *free?*"

"Of course. I can't watch a whole audience and Shakespeare all by myself, can I?"

He was wondering how to get rid of them for now. He was sure he could wrangle them free passes, once he explained the security angle. But he was already finding them tedious company, and he wanted to meet the show train on his own.

McArtle, bless him, solved the problem by consulting

35

his pocket watch. "We'd best get cracking, Phil," he said. "We got to get back and explain the situation to the marshal. After that there's barely time to sup and tell our wives afore we head over to the auditorium." He turned to Longarm and added, "Do you reckon we ought to show up early and sort of scout afore the doors open to the public, Longarm?"

Longarm said, "That's a damned good notion, Tom. Your badges ought to get you past the doorman. I'll meet you both there later, once I round up the Divine Sarah and her French dudes."

So they all parted friendlier than they'd met. Longarm knew that if he went back to the hotel to find Penny clean and naked he'd likely miss the train. So he went over to a beanery and filled his gut with steak and an order of fried hash on the side. He knew better than to order chili this far north. As he'd complained in Denver to no avail, they made chili just right in Pueblo, damn it. South of Pueblo it kept getting hotter and hotter in each trail town until, along the border, you could hardly get it down without bawling. While, north of Pueblo, chili kept getting weaker and weaker, till it got to tasting just like baked beans.

The train ride north had given him an appetite for some reason, so he had dessert. He solved the problem of deciding between mince and apple pie by having both, washed down with four mugs of Arbuckle. He had a notion he might want to stay awake this evening, no matter how things turned out.

Longarm and his fellow lawmen weren't the only folks who were waiting for the Divine Sarah to arrive in Cheyenne. As Longarm made his way to the railroad siding onto which the troupe train would be shunted from the main U. P. line, a brass band was already tuning up and more townsfolk than one could shake a stick at were gathered, peering down the still-deserted railroad tracks. Local politicians in duds pretty enough to be buried in were flapping back and forth like big black chickens. Most of the women in the crowd were dressed in their Sunday best, sensible dresses and silly

36

hats. But the madam and the girls from Cheyenne's fanciest parlor house had hired an open carriage to come over and see the fun while showing off their charms. The madam's charms threatened to spill over the front of her low-cut bodice any minute, and a uniformed Cheyenne copper was fussing at her about it. Longarm paid them no mind. Indecent exposure was not a federal offense, and he knew that the wicked gals would behave when push came to shove. They were funning the local fuddy-duddies, but they knew better than to disgrace Cheyenne in front of foreigners.

Some hands from off the surrounding range had ridden in to see what all the fuss was about and maybe to count the Divine Sarah's heads. They were joshing and saying mean things about fancy French dudes. But Longarm saw that most of them had shaved and some of them were wearing their fancy winter chaps and red kerchiefs. Longarm scanned the crowd for faces he might have seen on recent wanted fliers. He didn't see any. But one sort of sinister-looking gent in an undertaker's frock coat was leaning against a telegraph pole with a 12-gauge repeater cradled over one arm.

Longarm ambled over to ask him why. He asked politely, of course, introducing himself.

The gent with the scattergun said, "They told us someone like you would join the troupe here. I'm Brennen, U.P. police."

"I was hoping you were on my side. Are you expecting any trouble?" Longarm asked.

The railroad dick spat. "We're paid to see trouble *don't* happen. But it's costing that French gal extra. They wired from Omaha that she's mad as a wet hen and threatening to declare war when she gets back to France. The U.P. told her us railroad dicks are just as good as the sissy Secret Service when it comes to blowing outlaws off a moving train. But the Bernhardt woman seems to think it's an insult to lose her official federal bodyguard."

Longarm nodded. "She was promised as much. That's why I'm here. Can you tell me who I'm supposed to check in with when her train arrives?"

"Yep. Same gent I'm to meet. A dude called Dumont, from the Frog embassy in Washington. I'll be riding with you as far as Ogden. That's where the U.P. is off the hook. The Western Pacific will pick up her combo from there, and I can get back to serious business." He spat again. "Damned if I can see what all the fuss is about. Who in tarnation would want to hold up a mess of actors when there's all manner of payrolls and such rolling back and forth across South Pass?"

Before Longarm had to think up an answer, someone in the crowd shouted, "Here she comes!" And, sure enough, Longarm could see a smoke plume down the tracks to the east. He and the railroad dick moved over closer to the siding as a cowhand shouted, "Powder River and let her buck!" He only got to shoot his revolver at the sky twice before a Cheyenne copper stopped him.

There was no stopping the brass band. It commenced to play "La Marseillaise." They'd practiced it some, but since it wasn't every day the national treasure of France visited Cheyenne, they were a mite off-key. They made up for not knowing the song too well by playing it as loud as they could.

The sound of the band was almost drowned by a roar of angry frustration from the crowd as the U. P. locomotive puffed right past them on the main line instead of stopping in the siding. Longarm knew, of course, how one hired one's own train, so he didn't get upset.

Circus trains, theatrical-troupe trains, and specials hired by rich dudes weren't regular trains from cowcatcher to caboose. The railroads had better things to do with their serious rolling stock. So, if you asked nicely and paid well, they'd attach a section of private cars to a regular run that was going somewhere sensible, and drop your combo off on a siding like this one in Cheyenne before going on to meet the timetable. As Longarm expected, the U.P. transcontinental wheezed to a stop up the main line and then commenced to back Sarah Bernhardt's private section onto the siding. The Divine Sarah must have known how Yankee

38

railroads worked by this time, for she and some others of her troupe were standing on the observation platform of their rear car as it backed into the deafening roar of welcome from Cheyenne.

Longarm could see which one was the Divine Sarah long before she and her sidekicks were within pistol range. The leading lady stood dead center, waving graciously, while her underlings let her hold the invisible spotlight. She looked taller than the other gals and, come to think of it, taller than the men on either side as the train backed in. Longarm hadn't heard that the Divine Sarah was a giantess, so he figured she had to be standing on a box. He grinned when he saw the outfit she had on. Miss Bernhardt's head was bare, but her dress was a dead ringer for the one he'd peeled off Penelope Wayne that afternoon. He somehow doubted that Sarah Bernhardt aped the costume of aspiring young actresses, so he figured old Penny had somehow found a Denver seamstress who could whip up a copy of a dress she'd only seen in a theatrical magazine.

He made a mental note to talk to Penny about her duds before he brought her anywhere near the Divine Sarah. For such a she-male little gal, Penny sure had a poor grasp of she-male behavior. The *Police Gazette* allowed the Divine Sarah had a sort of passionate artistic temper, and many a minister's wife had been known to throw a fit when a younger gal turned up in church wearing a dress like the parson's wife's! He could see that there was more to managing aspiring actresses than he'd fully considered. Rehearsing love scenes with them wasn't all that rough. But from there on it could get complicated.

As the train hissed to a halt, a delegation of townies pressed forward to present the Divine Sarah with a mess of sunflowers, a gilt-wood key to the city and, for some reason, a ten-gallon sombrero. Sarah Bernhardt leaned over the rail to accept them graciously. She handed the key to Cheyenne to a gent who looked as though he was wondering what on earth to do with it. But she hung on to the sunflowers and put on the big cowboy hat as the crowd roared approval.

Longarm nudged the railroad dick and said, "Hell, she looks like a good sport, at least."

Brennen spat again. "She's just play-acting. In Iowa she raised holy hell 'cause we couldn't provide her with fish eggs. That's what she eats for breakfast. Black fish eggs. Ain't that a bitch?"

"You mean caviar? They serve caviar in Chicago. I had some once. It ain't bad. It ain't good, neither, but what the hell."

The railroad dick growled, "I don't care what they eats in Chicago. Nobody out *here* eats fish eggs. I hear that ain't all them French dudes eat. They say all Frenchmen fight with their feet and fuck with their mouths. I'll bet that old gal has somethin' interestin' to do while she swallows them fish eggs and—"

"Stop right there!" Longarm cut in. "Miss Sarah Bernhardt is a guest of the United States government. And it ain't polite to pass such remarks about any lady, guest or not!"

"Shit, she ain't no lady. She's an actress, and a Jew-gal besides!"

Longarm shook his head wearily and said, "I can see you ain't a fan of Shakespeare and likely are a member of the Know-Nothing Party, Brennen. But if you really mean to ride with us to Ogden, you're going to have to learn some toleration. Like I said, I was sent up here to make sure the national treasure of France don't get mistreated or insulted. And, as of now, I am on the job. I sure hope you follow my drift. I generally get along with the U.P. and I'd sure hate like hell to have to explain any missing teeth of yours to them."

Brennen's eyes snapped like whips as his face went ashen, got red, then paled again, while Longarm just met his stare with the polite expression of gun-metal eyes that meant what they said.

Brennen licked his lips and said, "A man's entitled to his opinion, ain't he?"

Longarm nodded. "It says so in the constitution. But if

you can't be polite to folk of the Hebrew persuasion no matter who *you* pray to, personal, you ain't no pro and I don't need you. There's likely at least one Jewish person here in Cheyenne for you to make a face at. But nobody's going to insult Miss Sarah Bernhardt about her faith while I'm on the job—to her face or behind her back. So what's it going to be?"

Brennen lowered his eyes, shifted the shotgun in his arms, and muttered, "Oh, hell, let's not fuss about it. I'm stuck with the chore as far as Ogden. The office car is forward."

Longarm nodded and they started up the track away from the crowd around the platform. Up ahead, they saw some stagehands sliding scenery out of a car onto a buckboard. But they didn't have to go around. Longarm spied a sign on a chain hung across the platform of a closer car. It read EMPLOYEES ONLY. He unhooked the chain and they climbed aboard.

Sure enough, the innards of the car were fixed up like an office at the end facing the entrance. Two gents inside were talking in French and waving their arms at one another. One prissy little man in a Prince Albert waxed mustache was standing. The other, bigger man was sitting with his butt hooked over the edge of a desk. Longarm had tried to pick up some French while shacked up with that Metis gal on the Peace River that time. But they were talking too fast for him to follow their drift and, like the Metis gal had told him, Canadian French wasn't much like Paris French.

They stopped when they spotted the two lawmen in the doorway. The bigger man stood up and spoke in English, with a British accent. "This is a private car, sirs," he said.

Longarm flashed his badge. "We know. That's why we came in. They call me Longarm and I'm from the Justice Department. This here's Brennen of the U. P. Which one of you gents might be the Mr. Dumont we're supposed to check in with?"

The tall Englishman laughed and said, "Fortunately for him, he got off in Omaha. I'm Edward Jarret, Madame

Sarah's manager. This is Monsieur Latour, our butler."

Longarm held out his hand to shake. Jarret shook, but the little Frenchman looked startled and drew back as though Longarm's hand were dirty. Jarret explained, "It's not their custom. I'm not familiar with your government customs, either. Are you from the Secret Service?"

Longarm hesitated as he sized the big Englishman up. Edward Jarret was about sixty or so and would have looked like an American's picture of a prissy English lord if he hadn't been so husky. His face was handsome enough for acting on stage, but his regular features were marred by an ugly blue scar on his right cheekbone. Longarm was tolerable at reading scars, and if someone somewhere in the past hadn't bounced a bullet off Edward Jarret's handsome face, Longarm had never seen powder burns before.

Jarret's pale blue eyes were knowing, so Longarm decided not to beat around the bush with him. "We've taken over from Secret Service," he said. "I'm a deputy U. S. marshal. You see, out here—"

"I see all too well," Jarret cut in. "Madame Sarah was well received in London this spring. Apparently the States are more prudish. The critics in New York savaged her. Frankly, we're losing money on this tour. I thought a swing west might recoup our losses, since you Westerners are supposed to be more tolerant than the jumped-up four hundred back east—but have a look at this."

He took a folded sheet of foolscap from the pocket of his frock coat and handed it to Longarm. Longarm unfolded it and read:

Dear Painted Whore,
   We don't want your kind in Utah. If you stick your long Jew nose over the South Pass we mean to cut it off. Real Americans don't fancy your kind, even when they don't sleep in coffins and feed live quail to their pet lions. Utah is a Christian land and we mean to keep it that way. This is your last warning.
                                A Mormon Gentile.

Longarm grimaced and handed the note to Brennen. He told Jarret, "That was written by some ignorant maniac out to scare you."

"They succeeded," Jarret said. "For the record, Madame Sarah does not sleep in a coffin. Madame Sarah does not feed quail or anything else to her pet lion, since she has no pet lion and loves all animals, including birds. Furthermore, while Madame Sarah is proud to admit she's half Jewish by birth, she happens to be a devout Roman Catholic. But if those fanatic Mormons in Utah are going to make trouble for us—"

"They ain't," said Longarm flatly. "Mormons come in all shapes and sizes, same as anyone else, and some can act as fanatic as a Holy Roller under a full moon. But no Mormon, fanatic or otherwise, wrote that fool threat. No Mormon would have signed himself a *gentile*. To the Latter-Day Saints, a gentile is anybody who ain't a Mormon— including Jews, Catholics, or Baptists. I'd say the note was an empty threat. For, if anyone living on the far side of the pass was laying for you, he'd know the local lingo better."

Jarret stared soberly at Longarm for a moment, then smiled charmingly. "I'm starting to feel better about you, Deputy. I can see you know your way about out here—and you just saved me from having to reroute our tour. But Madame Sarah is still going to be upset about your not being a Secret Service agent. She had her heart set on the same privileges your government accords other important visitors."

Longarm said, "I'd best meet up with her and do some explaining, then."

Jarret hesitated, then nodded. "I think you might, at that," he agreed. "She'll have finished waving to the crowd by now. Latour will show you to her private car. Brennen had best stay here with me for the moment. Madame has wired a declaration of war to the Union Pacific, and she can only absorb so much information at a time in English."

Jarret said something to the butler in French and Latour told Longarm to follow him.

Longarm had already seen the outside of the special, so he studied the interior as the Frenchman led him through. He already knew that the forward car held baggage and scenery, and he supposed the quarters and such Jarret had beyond his office was the Englishman's own business. Latour led him through a standard Pullman dining car and two cars built European-style with a corridor down one side and private compartments along the other. He made a mental note that the corridor would be facing north, going over the South Pass. He'd only be able to run up and down the side facing north if trouble came in the wild stretches past Bitter Creek. But since Indians and owlhoots generally attacked from off the right of way, it was better than if the corridor was facing south.

They got to the last car—an entire Pullman lounge and observation car made up for the Divine Sarah and her personal servants. It was divided into sleeping compartments and a small kitchen, forward. The rear half of the car was a big handsomely furnished salon. Wine velvet drapes had been drawn across the glass leading out to the observation platform. In the center of the imposing waste of space, Sarah Bernhardt, in Penelope Wayne's dress, sat in a straight-back chair. A motherly but handsome older woman stood behind her, fixing her hair.

Longarm took off his Stetson as the butler introduced him to Madame and her traveling companion, another Madame called Guerard, who smiled but didn't say much. Madame Sarah was staring at him like a wounded deer, but she managed to say that she was enchanted.

Longarm wasn't sure he was enchanted with her. Up close, the Divine Sarah was sort of disappointing at first glance. He'd figured from her pictures she was built slim. But the camera put a few pounds on a gal, and in the flesh she was a skinny little thing. Her face was as white as sunbleached buffalo bone and the hair Madame Guerard was fussing with was the color and consistency of the fuzz under a hotel bed. Her nose was too long and her chin was weak. The only pretty thing about her was her eyes. And those

44

eyes made up for a lot indeed. They were deep-set and smoldering with life and energy in her washed-out, consumptive face. They stared at him like hot coals as she asked him if he was a Secret Service man.

Longarm smiled down at her and said, "My department took you away from Treasury, ma'am. Washington figured you were too important to entrust to mere Secret Service. I'm a deputy U.S. marshal."

Sarah Bernhardt frowned. "I do not understand, Monsieur. It was my impression that your Secret Service guarded the lives of your president and his *très fatigué* First Lady, *non?*"

He said, "Yes, ma'am. That's 'cause they're only in the White House *temporary*. You see, the Secret Service is junior to us. It was only formed a few years back, during the War betwixt the States. The U.S. Marshal's Office has been working for Uncle Sam since old George Washington's time. That's why, when we heard you was coming, we insisted on the honor of bodyguarding you and yours."

Sarah Bernhardt clapped her hands and laughed like a little girl. Her laugh filled the coach with meadowlarks and butterflies and Longarm understood, finally, what all the fuss was about. The Divine Sarah pointed at a nearby ottoman and her magic voice tinkled like a brook in fairyland as she made an invitation to sit down sound important as hell.

Longarm lowered his butt to the low seat, leaning his elbows on his higher-than-usual knees. So now he had to look up at her on her throne. He knew she'd planned it that way, but he didn't care. She seemed to be a good sport, for a queen, and he enjoyed just listening to her magic voice. She was still too skinny—and no matter what Madame Guerard did to that frizzy hair, it would still be a mess—but if a man half closed his eyes, Sarah Bernhardt was Cleopatra and the gal you took home to Mother all in one.

Longarm had never met a gal more she-male, and he'd met many a gal in his time. He wondered how she did it. She didn't wiggle or bat her eyes, and her perfume was just ordinary stink-pretty, albeit likely expensive and French.

45

But he found himself gushing like an awkward schoolboy as he let her draw him out about the route ahead. She seemed to think there were lions and tigers and bears as well as Shoshone in the South Pass, and it made him feel like a knight in shining armor to assure her that the West wasn't all that much wilder than the East.

"I was in New York City a spell back, picking up a want for Leavenworth," he said. "They got mean folks everywhere, Miss Sarah. I'm sure the boys here in Cheyenne will admire you as much as I do."

She sighed. "Monsieur is *très gallant*. Alas, I know all too well how savage is New York. They called me 'The Bernhardt' and drew cruel cartoons about me in the newspapers. Tell me, Custis Long, do you think I am too thin?"

"Well, ma'am, I'd be a liar if I said you was fat. But there's nothing wrong with being—ah—sort of willowy."

"I have never been able to gain weight, no matter how much I eat. When I was a child I had consumption. That is one of the reasons I wished to tour your West. They say the air out here is good for the consumption, *non?*"

"Oh, sure, hardly anybody ever dies of consumption here in the High Country. But since you brung it up, and I'm supposed to look after you, do you reckon we ought to get you a doctor or a nurse to travel along with us? I'm allowed to sign for anything it takes to keep you safe and well."

She laughed her meadowlark laugh. *"Mais non,* but you are most thoughtful as well as gallant. I assure you, I am not ill. My face is this ashen shade partly because I avoid the sun and use Oriza face powder and partly, I confess, because I am suffering most dreadfully from . . . Do not look so concerned; I assure you it is not catching, unless one is an actor. I think you Americans call it stage fright."

Longarm looked incredulous. "I find that hard to believe, ma'am. Why, you've been a big stage star since . . . uh— whenever."

The Divine Sarah smiled with her big eyes and said, *"Oui,* it *has* been a long time since I first appeared in the Comédie Française. I have a son fifteen years old, back in France. So there is no need for awkward gallantry about my age, Custis, *mon cher*. But one never gets too old to feel frightened in a strange city. And, from what I have seen of Cheyenne so far, it is as strange a city as I have ever appeared in. Do you think they will enjoy my version of *King Lear*? We were hissed in Omaha."

Longarm shrugged and said, "I can't speak for them farmers further east, ma'am. Out here, it ain't considered polite to hiss a lady. To tell you true, I doubt many of the hands are all that familiar with Shakespeare and some of the big words might throw them. But you talk so pretty, I don't reckon it'll matter."

Sarah Bernhardt frowned. "Big words? Do you mean *English* words, Custis?"

"Well, sure. Shakespeare wrote the play in English, didn't he?"

She looked stricken and gasped, *"Quelle horreur!* I thought everyone understood we were presenting the play in French, of course."

Longarm didn't answer. He was stumped. Like many self-educated men, he'd taken the trouble to read some Shakespeare in his time, just to see what all the fuss was about. But some of the locals might not have, and *King Lear* was a mighty murky play even when you understood half of what in thunder was going on. Trying to follow the plot in French was going to be a chore for the cowhands, railroad workers, and such in Cheyenne.

Sarah Bernhardt was as good at reading eyes as she was at talking with her own. She moaned and told her companion, "I need some laudanum. We are lost! I can't go on. Suicide is the only way out."

Madame Guerard just went on combing Madame Sarah's hair as she asked Longarm, in a pleasant but plain human voice, to tell Madame Sarah that things couldn't be as bad as all that.

He nodded. "Folks have come from far and near to see you perform, ma'am. They know you're French and— shucks, *King Lear*'s hard to follow in English, too!"

It turned out wrong. Sarah Bernhardt covered her face with her tiny manicured hands and sobbed, "It is no use! You are right! *King Lear* is not for Wyoming Territory! Oh, *mon Dieu,* what am I to do?"

Longarm said, "Well, it ain't for me to say—but, since you ask, don't you have a favorite play you'd feel more comfortable with?"

The Divine Sarah didn't answer, but Madame Guerard did. "Of course she does. She can play *La Dame aux camélias* in her sleep. But she has always been a stubborn child."

Sarah Bernhardt sobbed. *"Merde alors,* I can't stage *that* old chestnut again! I must have died as Dame Gautier a hundred times by now and I wanted something *fresh* for my American audiences!"

Longarm frowned and asked, "Are you talking about the play *Camille?*"

The Divine Sarah put her hands down to laugh impishly and tell him, "That's so silly, Custis *mon cher!* There is nobody named Camille in the play! The lady of the camellias is named Marguerite Gautier and they call her the lady of the camellias, not Camille!"

"They do over here, ma'am. Miss Ellen Terry was a smash hit in *Camille* when I was in New York that time. Everybody enjoys a good cry—even cowhands. If I was you, and knowed *Camille* by heart, that's the play *I'd* put on for Cheyenne!"

Sarah Bernhardt looked thoughtful, even hopeful for a moment. Then her big eyes got sad again and she said, "It is too late. The playbills are posted, and by now they are erecting the scenery for *King Lear* at the theater. We shall have to leave for there any moment and—how you say?—face the music. Oh, I wish I had spoken to you sooner, Custis, *mon cher!* You are both so right! My troupe knows *La Dame aux camélias* as well as I, but, alas..."

"Look," he cut in, "you just go ahead and stage *Camille,* hear? Nobody here in Wyoming will notice if the scenery is a mite off. Shucks, they've never seen either play. What difference could it make?"

For some reason, that made both of the Frenchwomen laugh like hell. Sarah jumped up, danced over to Longarm, and bent to hold his cheeks in her tiny hands as she bent to kiss him smack on the mouth. "I am transfigured!" she said. "But now you must go, *mon cher*. I must turn into *La Dame aux camélias* in privacy, *non*?"

He said that sounded reasonable and got up to leave, his lips still tingling. That little French gal could *kiss!* He said he'd meet them over at the Civic Auditorium after he tended some chores.

Madame Guerard followed Longarm and Latour out. On the platform between the cars, she spun Longarm around and kissed him, too. He smiled down at her uncertainly and asked, "Ma'am?"

"That was for the way you rescued Madame from the depths of despair," she said. "She only talks about suicide, but she is not in good health, and we are grateful for the way you raised her spirits just now. Monsieur Jarret showed you the cruel note someone sent from Utah?"

"Yes, ma'am. I told him not to worry about it. I get along tolerable with Mormon folk, and they ain't like the rascal who sent that threat. But I'd best be on my way now—just in case there *are* any lunatics about, I mean to scout the auditorium some before you all open tonight."

As they made their way forward, Longarm noticed that the snooty little butler was acting friendlier, too. He said, "I know this ain't my business, Latour, but I couldn't help noticing that your manager, Jarret, seems to have met up with a bullet at close range in his time."

The Frenchman nodded. *"Oui.* Monsieur Jarret is *très formidable* when forced to defend a woman. He carries a gun under his coat, and he knows how to use it. He got that scar defending Miss Jenny Lind, the Swedish Nightingale, against the advances of a theatrical agent who— how you say—tried to take advantage of her?"

Longarm whistled and observed, "They surely must have had a serious discussion!"

Latour said, "They did. Monsieur Jarret was ready to settle the matter with fists. But the other drew a gun and

49

shot him in the face at point-blank range. Fortunately for Monsieur Jarret, the bullet glanced off his strong bone. The other man was less fortunate when Monsieur Jarret drew his own revolver. Naturally, the coroner's jury decided it was self-defense. Since then, few men have trifled with any female clients of Monsieur Jarret."

Longarm nodded. He'd thought the big Englishman looked tougher than the duds he wore. He made a mental note to warn Brennen about making any nasty cracks around the Divine Sarah's manager. He made another mental note that, if push came to shove, he could likely count on Jarret to hold steady under fire. A man who could still draw and fire after being shot in the face was no sissy.

Chapter 4

Longarm found Brennen alone in the office car. Jarret had gone on to the auditorium to supervise the scenery construction. The butler left them to their own devices.

Longarm told Brennen he was going into town, and added, "You'd best stay here and guard the rolling stock for the U.P. You've already been told Miss Sarah ain't exactly Jewish. But if it still bothers you, keep it to yourself. They tell me Jarret has sand in his craw—and he tends to get moody when gents insult ladies around him."

"I noticed," Brennen said. "We just had words. But I smoothed it over. I ain't looking for trouble, and I can see the Jews have you all fooled for now. In time to come, you'll see I was right. Them rabbits is sneaky as hell."

Longarm frowned. "Rabbits?"

Brennen nodded and said, "Yeah, that's what the Jews calls their leaders—rabbits. Haven't you ever read the Prodigals of Zion, Longarm?"

"Not hardly. I remember a prodigal son in the Good Book. I disremember him coming from Salt Lake City, though."

"Hell, the Prodigals of Zion wasn't writ by Mormons, it was writ by rabbits, over to Russia. The Russian Secret

51

Police found a copy and printed it up as a warning to the rest of us. According to the Prodigals of Zion, the Jew rabbits is plotting to take over the world in a few years."

Longarm muttered, "Oh, for God's sake," and left Brennen to brood as he headed back to the main drag.

He stopped at the telegraph office and wired Billy Vail that he'd been piped aboard and the war about Secret Service was over. Then, since Brennen and the other lunatic who'd sent the anti-Jewish note had reminded him that some folks had dumb notions indeed, he sent some other wires. The Know-Nothing Party and the Klan hadn't been acting worse than usual to Jewish folk so far this year. But, not being Jewish, Longarm figured he might have missed the opening shots if another tedious outburst was afoot. Rabbi Levine at the Denver Temple would likely know if anything really ugly was up.

He went back to the hotel. It was dark out now. Penny was combing her hair in front of the mirror in their hired room. She was wearing the same dress he'd just seen Sarah Bernhardt wearing. He sat on the bed and asked her if she had something else to wear to the performance.

Penny said, "No. This is my very best dress. And I was starting to worry about you, darling. Where have you been all this time? The play starts at eight, and we've barely time to get there!"

He filled her in on his adventures so far—or tried to. But when he got to the part about meeting the Divine Sarah, Penny cut in to demand, "Did you tell her about me?"

He said, "Not yet. Things were sort of hectic over to the train. I'll carry you over to the auditorium and buy you a ticket. Then, later—"

"Buy me a ticket!" she wailed. "Oh, how could you humiliate me so? I'm not a member of the public. I'm an *actress!* Surely you have the influence to get me backstage, dearest?"

He shrugged. "I don't know. It never came up. Look, Penny, I seem to get along with Miss Sarah, tolerable. I will be wandering about behint the scenery and everywhere else I can check out while the performance is going on. But I don't want you tagging along in that fool dress. Why don't you just sit out front in the audience and when the show's over and everybody starts to leave, you can naturally hang about as my gal and we can play it by ear."

"Oh, you mean there'll be a cast party in the green room, later?"

"Honey, I don't know what I mean. I'm a U.S. deputy, not a theatergoer. I said we'd play her by ear. But we'd best get cracking. You're right about it getting late, and I want to poke about some before the curtain rises."

She put on her silly hat and he escorted her on foot to the Civic Auditorium. The ticket office was open, so he bought her a ticket in the orchestra section when she asked him to. But the doors weren't open to the public yet. He hesitated, then said, "You stay here till they let you in. I'm going around to the stage door."

"I want to go with you, damn it!"

"I know you do. But you can't. I mean it, Penny. I said I'd try to help you with your career if I could, but that ain't what I was sent up here to do, and if you don't stop acting so eager, you'll ruin your own chances. I told you I already met Miss Sarah and her manager, and they seem neighborly. But they must get pestered half to death by gals like you, and the only way you'll keep them from thinking you're a stagestruck ninny is to stop acting like one, hear? You just wait till the doors open and go on in like a regular human being. Then I'll recognize you after the play and call you out of the crowd. That dress is likely to start a war with Madame Sarah. So if I can introduce you to Jarret, just behave yourself and let me do the talking. I mean to introduce you as a famous American actress I know from Denver, see?"

"Do you think it will work?"

"The odds are fifty-fifty. But that's better than you'd do on your own, wearing that tactical error and acting too pushy. I have to go, honey. I'll see you after the show."

He left her by the box office and circled around to the

alley leading to the stage door. He saw the stage door was open and when he got to it the doorman knew his name and made no fuss about him walking right in. The Divine Sarah and her French troupe had beat him there. The little star was in her dressing room putting on more chalky powder or something. But he spied Jarret standing by some ropes, talking to McArtle from the Cheyenne marshal's office. As he joined them, McArtle said, "Your notion was a good one, Longarm. Look what we found under the stage when you sent us over early."

He held up a pasteboard shoe box. "Me and Woods found this taped to the boards under the stage." Then he lifted the lid and a big gray cat rolled over in Longarm's guts. A cheap brass clock was ticking above a bundle of sixty-percent dynamite sticks.

McArtle said, "It's defused, of course. According to Mr. Jarret, here, it was set to go off halfway through the play. Ain't that a bitch?"

"It would have been. Where's your sidekick, Woods, right now?"

"Staked out under the stage. We're hoping whoever planted this infernal device might come back to see why it never went off."

Longarm nodded. He knew that if *he'd* set a time bomb anywhere he wouldn't go near it, after. But, on the other hand, who but a maniac could guess what another might or might not do? As long as a deputy with a gun was posted under the stage, nobody was about to set another bomb ticking down there in the dark. McArtle said he'd best get rid of the fool thing and asked Longarm where he should post himself. Longarm said he'd take charge of the infernal device and suggested that McArtle post himself up above the audience with the limelight crew. So McArtle handed him the box and left him alone with Jarret. Longarm started taking the infernal device apart. He said to Jarret, "I was wondering why the front doors were still shut. It's up to you whether the show goes on or not."

Jarret called to a passing stagehand and told him to let

the savages in. He turned back to Longarm and said, "We have no choice, since so many tickets have been sold in advance. I say, I'm very grateful to you, Longarm. I fear I misjudged your police skills when first we met. You never mentioned you had gone to so much trouble on Madame's behalf."

Longarm shrugged modestly as he cursed himself for an idiot. He had, of course, only sent the two local deputies on what he'd thought would be a fool's errand, to get them out of his hair. He made a mental note to follow the same procedure at the next stop. For there was more than a crank letter to worry about now. Someone was really out to get the Divine Sarah. He asked Jarret if she knew. "Of course not," Jarret said. "I'll have to tell her later. But she's already in a terrible flap. She suffers terribly from stage fright as it is. If she thought someone in the audience was out to kill her—"

"That could still happen," Longarm cut in. "McArtle and I will be watching the audience, but we have to be realistic. What would happen if you folks just called off this tour?"

Jarret shrugged. "We'd go broke, of course. Madame only made this trip across the Atlantic because she needs the money. She's a famous actress in France, but the French are not big spenders, and Madame has a habit of living beyond her income. Aside from sending her love child to the best schools and supporting dozens of less worthy friends and relations, Madame incurred huge debts during the Franco-Prussian War."

"That was quite a few years ago, wasn't it?"

"It was. During the fighting, Madame took it into her head to follow the troops with her own field hospital. She saved many lives. She made no distinction between the French and German wounded she and her nurses picked up off the battlefields. She hoped, in time, to be reimbursed for her expenses by the Emperor Napoleon, but, since he lost . . ."

"I follow your drift. But are they still dunning her for bandages and such at this late date?"

"They are. She borrowed money from Swiss bankers to fund her field hospital. The gnomes of Zurich are *très pratique* about collecting their debts with interest. This tour might have got Madame off the hook, if it had gone as well as we'd hoped. Up until now, it's been a disaster."

"She told me as much. I don't savvy this stage fright business, Jarret. How come the Divine Sarah suffers stage fright this late in the game?"

"She's a great actress," Jarret answered simply. "I've handled everything from flea circuses on up the line in my time, and it's a funny thing. Only terrible actors and actresses are sure enough of themselves to step out there without butterflies in their stomachs. A really good actor knows how many things can go wrong."

Longarm nodded, but before he could say anything, music started playing somewhere and Sarah Bernhardt joined them, looking like death warmed over in skull-white makeup and a filmy dress that could have doubled as a funeral shroud. She nodded sadly to Longarm, then turned to Jarret and sobbed, "I can't go on! I am going to faint! The play is too long. I shall never last long enough to die properly."

Jarret took the tiny woman in his bearish arms, kissed her lightly on the cheek, and said, "You've never fainted on stage yet unless you planned to. The curtain's going up. Get out there and break a leg, you silly!"

"I can't! I won't!" wailed Sarah Bernhardt. Then, as the curtain began to rise and the audience began to applaud, she straightened up like a little soldier and marched out into the limelight to face them.

Longarm unbuttoned his frock coat in case he needed to get at his cross-draw rig. He moved away from Jarret as the manager went on standing there in the wings. Longarm couldn't see the crowd out front at all from that position. He found a stairway and mounted the steps to a perch behind some dummy organ pipes where he could look out and down at the audience below. He looked for Penny's cherry hat in the orchestra section but failed to spot it. She'd likely taken if off so the folks behind her could see. There were half a

56

dozen blonde heads down there in the dim light.

The stage was lit up swell as the Divine Sarah half re-
clined on a sofa jawing with some dude in French. The
Wyoming folk tittered. Save for a few Canuck trappers down
there, hardly any of them could understand a word. But, as
the lady of the camellias filled the auditorium with her magic
voice, the crowd settled down to watch what was going on.
You didn't have to understand French to sense that something mighty important was taking place up there.

Longarm chuckled fondly as he watched Madame Sarah
win them over. From up here, she looked pretty as hell,
and any fool cowhand could see that the poor thing was
unhappy and likely dying of something awful. But he hadn't
climbed up here to watch the play. He was out to make sure
there were no unseemly interruptions.

The house was packed almost solid, with only a seat
empty here and there. The audience sat quiet and rapt, like
kids hearing a fairy tale and straining to make out the bigger
words they didn't quite understand. He saw some buckskin
and hickory shirts toward the back, in the cheaper seats.
When one fool called out, "Hey, which one's King Lear?"
a cowhand sitting behind him whipped his Stetson across
the back of his neck and warned him to shut up.

To Longarm's surprise, he was able to follow the story,
even spoken in French much faster and pitched much higher
than they spoke it up Canada way. The plot was simple.
Old Marguerite was in love and wanted to get hitched, but
she had some kind of disease and didn't think it was fair
to her beloved. He was being a good sport about it and
would have married her anyway, but the lady of the camellias wouldn't hear of it. Somewhere in the audience, a
gal started bawling fit to bust. Even grown cowhands were
wiping at their faces surreptitiously. Nobody in Cheyenne
had enjoyed such a good cry since the Sioux gave up in
'76.

Longarm already knew that Madame Sarah was fixing
to die at the end of the play—but he never got to see her
do so that night. He heard two distant shotgun blasts and

57

was moving down the steps even before the audience began to murmur, uneasily, then settled back to watch some more. If the Divine Sarah had heard the gunshots, she never let on. She just kept on dying.

Longarm met Jarret down by the stage door. The Englishman had a big Webley revolver in one fist, so Longarm knew he'd heard the gunshots, too.

Jarret snapped, "They came from the alley out back, I think."

Longarm nodded, drew his own .44, and, since the doorman had locked the stage door and gone off somewhere, Longarm drew the bolt himself and slid the big steel-clad door open. He moved out quickly and got out of the light from behind him. Jarret did the same on the other side. As the two men stared into the darkness, letting their eyes adjust, Jarret said, "It's clear to the street, I think. What's that on the pavement ahead?"

"Cover me. I'll find out," said Longarm, and moved forward, squinting at the pale still shape on the ground. As he got closer, he moaned. "Oh, no! That ain't *fair*, Lord!"

Penelope Wayne lay face down on the gritty pavement with her cherry hat spilled a few feet away and a big wet patch of dark blood spoiling the back of her familiar dress.

Longarm knelt to feel the side of Penny's throat. There was no pulse. He hadn't expected any. Damned few folks went on breathing after being blasted twice in the back with a shotgun.

Edward Jarret came to join Longarm, saying that Deputy McArtle was covering them from the stage door. When he saw what Longarm had found, he gasped. "My God! Who could that be—and what she doing out here in the alley?"

Longarm stood up. "Her name was Penny. She wanted to be an actress. She was here in the alley because she hoped to meet Miss Sarah. I'd bought her a seat inside, but she likely got impatient and took the bit between her teeth."

"Why would anyone want to shoot her if she was a harmless, stagestruck kid?"

"Take a look at the dress she's wearing."

Jarret bent to peer closer, blanched, and said, "Oh, no! She was wearing a dress like the one Madame Sarah was wearing when we first arrived."

"There you go. By now that infernal device would have gone off, if them other deputies had not found it. The killers were the bombers. They were lurking out here, hoping to hear some noise. Instead, they saw what looked like Sarah Bernhardt in the dim light. They figured we'd found and defused the bomb. They figured you'd probably sent an understudy on while the real Sarah Bernhardt slipped out the back to safety. By now they're long gone, but we can safely assume they have no confederates in the audience inside. They'd have known the real McCoy was dying on stage right now, so Penny wouldn't have died out here!"

They heard police whistles, a couple of dark figures appeared at the alley entrance. Longarm called out, "Over here, boys. Don't get excited about this gun in my hand and I won't get excited about yours. We're all law here."

Two Cheyenne lawmen came to join them and Longarm filled them in before asking them if they'd get the meat wagon and carry Penny's cadaver to the morgue. They said they would, so Longarm took Jarret by the arm and said, "We'd best go back in and lock that door."

Jarret nodded. "You're right. I'll have to tell Madame Sarah later, but not until after her final curtain call. She's already on the thin edge of hysteria."

"Do tell? I thought she had the audience licking out of her little hand."

"That's when she's most apt to fall apart. You're right about the house tonight. They've been angels so far. But that's when Madame Sarah is most afraid of them. As any actress knows, the audience is a beast that can turn on you any moment. It's when she loves them, as she does tonight, that it really hurts."

Chapter 5

Sarah Bernhardt brought down the house in Cheyenne that night. She took curtain call after curtain call. The crowd was enchanted to find she hadn't really died in the last act after all, but was risen from the dead to blow them kisses with tears running down both cheeks as they clapped and stomped and hollered. The mayor, the local chapter of the D. A. R., and the Cheyenne Volunteer Fire Department had already given her flowers earlier. But they managed another cartload between them, while others in the audience threw posies until the Divine Sarah stood there in her shroud, ankle deep in flowers and half hidden by the blizzard of blooms. They wouldn't let her off the stage until she gave them more of her magic. So, seeing that Camille had already died once that evening, she held up an imperious hand for silence and recited "Deux pigeons s'aimaient d'amour tendre," for them, after explaining in English that the sort of dumb poem about two pigeons in love was the first thing she'd ever recited on stage, at the age of fifteen. Few of the Cheyenne folk understood the words, but they grasped her sentimental gesture, and everyone was so touched that the mayor's wife invited her to join the local chapter of the D. A. R. Some ladies who'd vowed they would never serve tea to an actress under any circumstances seconded the motion.

Longarm didn't get to see any of that. Knowing that McArtle, Woods, and the tough old Jarret could get Madame Sarah and the others safely back to the train through anything less than a Sioux uprising, he'd lit out to tidy up after the killing of Penny Wayne and tend some other chores while there was time. Jarret had told him that the troupe would be leaving town shortly after midnight.

The coroner had been at the performance with his wife, but Longarm found an assistant willing to sign Penny's death certificate as murder by person or persons unknown. They agreed that there was no call to hold any member of Madame Sarah's troupe as a witness, since nobody inside the auditorium had seen the killing.

Longarm didn't know Penny's Denver address. But, going through her things after he'd brought them over from the hotel, he and the assistant coroner found some letters to her from home. As he'd suspected, Penny was more a farmer's daughter than an actress. Her folks had indulged her in her dream, and she'd left a bitty crossroads town in Kansas to pursue it. The coroner's assistant said he'd get in touch with Penny's folks so they could send for her remains if they wanted to. In the meantime, she'd keep a spell, embalmed with arsenic. The law was starting to frown on arsenic embalming in most states of late, but Wyoming was still a territory and it hardly seemed likely that Penny had died of poison.

Leaving the morgue, Longarm headed for the Western Union office near the depot. The streets were deserted for such an early hour. Most of Cheyenne was either over at the auditorium or drinking in the saloons. The telegraph clerk had some return wires for him. Longarm stuffed them into his coat pocket to read later as he sent another telegram to Billy Vail, bringing him up to date on the killing, the attempted bombing, and the fact that Sarah Bernhardt had some enemies beyond what was normal for any famous person.

When he'd sent the telegram, Longarm consulted his watch and, knowing the troupe hadn't left the auditorium yet, decided to scout the railroad siding, unexpected.

There were streetlamps in the center of town, but they started to peter out as he walked down the tracks toward the railyards. His shadow walked ahead of him on the cinder path and got longer and longer as he spied the special ahead. There were slits of light through the curtains of the Pullman varnish cars. He knew the servants and such were still aboard, along with the U. P. dick, Brennen, so he didn't worry about the danger of untended lamps inside. He was just abreast of the forward baggage and scenery car when someone yelled, "Longarm! Behind you!"

Longarm didn't waste time looking back or asking who'd shouted the warning. He threw himself sideways and rolled under the baggage car as shots rang out in the night from both sides—with him in the middle.

Longarm crawled up behind one truck of the car under-which he'd sheltered, his own gun drawn, and risked a peek around the steel wheel as the gunplay fell silent. A voice he now recognized as Brennen's called out, "Are you all right, Longarm?"

"Yeah. I'm under the car," he called back. "Where are you, and who are we having this fuss with?"

"I'm directly above you. Forward platform. I think I got him. I was smoking in the shade of the overhang and seen you coming. You had company following, and when I seen him go for his gun—"

"Thanks, I see him now. There's a bump on the cinder path I disremember stepping over, coming down it. Cover me. I'll have a look-see."

But Brennen dropped down off the platform ahead of Longarm and called back, *"You* cover *me!* The son of a bitch is on *railroad* property, dead or alive!"

That sounded a lot more sensible than moving in on a downed man in tricky light. So Longarm covered Brennen as the railroad dick crunched back along the path to the mysterious bump and kicked it a couple of times. "He's

63

dead. *That'll* larn the son of a bitch!" Brennen said.

Longarm rolled out from under the car and got to his feet. Behind him, someone opened a door and called out in French. Longarm yelled in English to get back inside, and the servant must have savvied, for the door shut with a slam.

He joined Brennen as the railroad dick had knelt and struck a match above the face of the corpse on the path. A nondescript face Longarm had never seen before was staring glassily up at the flickering light. A long-barreled dragoon .45 lay between the body and an upside-down black Stetson on the cinders.

Brennen said, "He ain't on my list. How about yourn?"

Longarm knelt and started going through the cadaver's pockets. The match burned down to Brennen's fingers and the railroad dick shook it out with a curse. Longarm found the dead man's wallet. "Strike another light, will you?" he asked. Brennen did. The wallet contained twenty-two dollars and a ticket to Ogden, Utah, on the coach. There was a card with the name of one Wilbur Smith, Denver, Colorado. That would be easy enough to check out by wire. Longarm and Brennen stood up. Brennen said something dumb about getting the coroner, but Longarm shook his head. "I don't want to confuse Cheyenne no more. Ed Jarret says this special will be picked up shortly after midnight and, what the hell, this rascal was shot on railroad property by a railroad dick. We can stow him in the baggage car for now. When we get to Ogden, you can turn him over to the law there and do the paperwork, since that's where you'll be getting off for keeps, in any case. I owe you, Brennen. It *smarts* to get hit in the back with a .45!"

Brennen shrugged. "Just doing my job. Why do you reckon he was after you, Longarm? Could he be one of the rascals as shot that gal over to the theater, earlier?"

"Don't know. She was hit with a shotgun."

"Yeah, that's what they told me. But this rascal might not have wanted to draw notice, wandering about after you with a shotgun in his hands. Or there could have been two of 'em, and—"

"Who told you about the killing at the theater, Brennen?" Longarm cut in. "I've got a reason for asking."

Brennen shrugged. "Hell, I never asked his name. He just told me, mebbe an hour ago, in passing. I was sitting up there on the platform, smoking, and this bird come down the path, spotted me, and asked had I heard about the shooting."

"Was it someone from the special?"

"No. He talked American. I took him for a yard worker. I never thought to ask his name, damn it. He seemed to be just a good old boy passing on the latest gossip. What's eating you, Longarm? Half the folk in Cheyenne must have heard about the shooting by now, right?"

"Wrong. We kept it quiet. Save for me, Jarret, and the other lawmen, nobody in town but Miss Wayne's killer or killers should have known she was dead."

Brennen whistled thoughtfully, then said, "Well, I doubt like hell a killer would brag on it to the first gent he spied smoking a cigar in the night. Try her this way. The gossip was just some old boy coming from town who'd got the tale from someone he knowed on the Cheyenne police force."

Longarm nodded. "Makes sense. Let's pick this bastard up and get him out of sight before some other talkative copper comes along."

They put the hat and pistol aboard the cadaver's lap. Then Longarm took the shoulders and Brennen took the knees and they carried the body back to the baggage car and manhandled it onto the platform. Longarm tried the door. It was locked. He swore. "He'll keep here till we get the key. Jarret will want to know, in any case. Since he's been traveling all this while with Madame Sarah, he might even know the bastard on sight."

"His card hails him from Denver, Longarm."

"It calls him Smith, too. And somebody who don't talk Mormon claimed in a spite note to be from Utah. Members of the Know-Nothings have been known to fib about their identity."

As they stood on the platform with the corpse at their feet, Longarm fished out a cheroot and struck his own match to light it. He spotted the railroad dick's pump gun leaning in a corner. He waited until he had his smoke going before he asked, "How come you used your pisolivier on this gent, Brennen?"

Brennen said, "Hell, you can't hit anything that fur off with a scattergun. I only use old Betsy at close quarters. Besides, I just cleaned her this morning and I hates cleaning a repeater action."

He picked up the gun and handed it to Longarm as he added, sort of proudly, "She's a good old scattergun, but a mite delicate. You ever handle one of these newfangled repeaters, Longarm?"

Longarm hefted the repeater as if he gave a damn and put it back down, saying, "Yeah. I favors a Winchester, myself. I wonder what's keeping Madame Sarah and the others? It's getting late."

"The locomotive won't be here for a couple of hours," Brennen said. "I've been meaning to ask you. You keep mentioning this here Know-Nothing Party, Longarm. You even intimated I belonged to it. What in hell is a Know-Nothing?"

"Don't you know about them? I reckon, like me, you was just a nipper when they got started, back before the War. The Know-Nothing Party was started by folks spooked by all the Irish and German immigrants arriving in great numbers about mid-century. When all them people fleeing from the Irish Famine and the German revolution of '48 started arriving all at once, the Know-Nothing Party was formed to defend the red, white, and blue from praying Catholic or talking German. They spearheaded some ugly riots back East. But after a time the movement lost steam and most of the original members dropped out and joined more sensible parties, like the Republicans and such. Anyone with a lick of sense could see that the second generation of foreigners was growing up American. So when the Pope didn't run for President, and the Germans all learned English, nobody but a few fanatics stayed with the Know-Nothings."

66

He pointed down at the corpse on the platform. "The ones still fighting for the lost cause are hard-core lunatics, of course. If this gent was one of the killers at the auditorium, he likely hated foreigners past common sense. Everybody else who's met Madame Sarah seems to admire her. And, what the hell, it ain't like she plans to stay here and make us all learn French in our old age."

Brennen spat over the side and said, "Well, I never heard of the Know-Nothings, but I still don't trust them Jew rabbits. But hold on. You said *if* this jasper was a Know-Nothing. Don't you *know?*"

"Not hardly. They're called the Know-Nothings 'cause they never tell nobody nothing. I've been a deputy marshal quite a few years now, and I shot two men in Denver just before I came up here. This gent could have been after me, *personal!*"

"I'm sure glad I'll be getting off in Ogden tomorrow," Brennen said. "This game's getting a mite rich for my blood. It was bad enough when I only had to worry about someone murdering that skinny Jew gal under my nose. Now you tell me there's folks gunning for you, too."

Before Longarm could answer, they heard voices from the direction of town. The Divine Sarah and her troupe were coming down the path, escorted by a torchlit procession surrounding Madame's carriage. Longarm said to Brennen, "Stand beside me, like so. I don't want the ladies to see what we have on the deck."

Their shadows hid the corpse as the Divine Sarah's carriage passed. Longarm spied Jarret walking and hailed him over. As the tall Englishman joined them, Longarm filled him in and asked him to have a look at the dead man. Jarret did so, cursed a blue streak, and said he'd never seen the man before.

Longarm got Jarret to unlock the baggage-car door and they rolled the late Wilbur Smith inside. Jarret said he'd see his stagehands about a tarp to cover the cadaver and agreed he'd keep until morning in the cool night air of the high country. Then he said he had to rejoin Madame and make sure she didn't invite half of Cheyenne to ride with them over the South Pass. The warm-natured actress was excited about the people of Cheyenne falling in love with her, after the way she'd been hissed in less civilized parts.

Longarm said that sounded sensible of Jarret. But, before the big Englishman left, Longarm asked him if the money they'd made that night would be riding with them aboard the train. Jarret shook his head and explained, "I banked the box office receipts here in Cheyenne, and got a certified cashier's check which only I can cash. I arranged it with them ahead of time."

Longarm said that sounded sensible, too, but added, "I couldn't help noticing that Madame Sarah had some mighty fancy jewelry on and about her person in her quarters. Are they real?"

Jarret nodded. "I tried to talk her out of wearing her jewels to America. But Sarah is stubborn. The only gem she really values is the Tear of Alexandre Dumas. She'd die if she lost that. The others, I suppose, could be replaced. People are always giving her new jewelry."

"Can you put a figure on how much her play-pretties might be worth to a no-questions jeweler, Jarret?"

Jarret shrugged. "I really don't know. A quarter of a million or so, perhaps."

"Jesus, she's packing a quarter of a million dollars' worth of jewelry?"

"No, a quarter of a million *pounds'* worth. Why?"

"Oh, Lord, what's an English pound worth in U.S. dollars these days?"

"Roughly five to one. I tried to get her to leave them in a safe back home. But you may have noticed that she's casual about her belongings. Madame Guerard picks up after her, of course, but Sarah's dreadfully careless. She's already lost a strand of pearls on this trip, God knows where. We almost took her New York hotel room apart looking for them, but..."

"I get the picture," Longarm said. "You go on back and calm her down. I'll join you all directly."

Jarret left, and Longarm turned to Brennen. "Well, you

heard that. Where do you reckon any owlhoots might try to hit us as we head over the pass?"

"Not this side of Bitter Creek. It's too settled. Past Bitter Creek the country grows more hair on its chest. Track threads through lots of aspen, crossing the headwaters of the Green River. If I was out to rob the U.P. I'd hit somewheres betwixt Bitter Creek and the Church Buttes. Then I'd ride like hell, north or south. It's all rough and empty country."

Longarm nodded. "I met the Shoshone up that way a few years back, so I know what you mean. Great minds run in the same channels, and if you and me see her that way, the owlhoots who know the country might, too. I want you riding the tender with the engine crew. I'll post myself on the rear observation platform. That's where they'll try to board, horseback, if they don't try to stop the train."

Brennen asked, "How in hell will we communicate with the whole damn train betwixt us, Longarm?"

"By gunshot, of course," Longarm answered. "You know the run, so you'll likely be alert to cuts and such where they might try to stop us. Old Jarret's handy with a gun, too. Maybe he knows some other men in the troupe he can count on in a fight. I'll work it out with him later. With you up in the tender, me on the rear platform, and Jarret prowling the corridor with that big English revolver, we can make 'em work at it if anyone's laying for us."

"Damn it, Longarm, three guns ain't enough! Can't you rustle up some more deputies here in Cheyenne?"

"I could if we knew for certain that someone planned to rob the train. But I don't like to cry wolf unless I see one. I ain't expecting train robbers and the Indians are quiet this summer."

"Then why are you spooking me with all this talk about guarding agin such happenings?"

Longarm smiled thinly and said, "I don't cry wolf, but I don't leave the henhouse door unlocked and open, either. We'll jaw about it later, after the U.P. picks us up. I gotta go congratulate the Divine Sarah on *her* performance tonight."

Chapter 6

Longarm found Jarret, Madame Guerard, and Sarah Bernhardt in the salon of the star's private car. Jarret was seated at a table, writing. Madame Guerard was knitting in a corner, as quiet as usual. Sarah Bernhardt had changed into a blue silk wrap and was modeling a clay head on a stand as she stood beside it, shifting her weight from one foot to the other like a little girl.

She brightened when she saw Longarm. "Oh, *mon cher* Custis, you were so right about the play! Did you hear the way I made them cry? Sit down; we were about to have refreshments. What do you think of my sculpture?"

Longarm found a chair and sat, hat in his lap, as he stared soberly at the bust the little Frenchwoman was working on. It looked like a boy in his early teens. He said, "You're mighty handy with that clay, ma'am. I didn't know you were artistic that way, too."

She lowered her lashes modestly. *"Merci.* It is the bust of my Maurice, done from memory. I miss my son so. I wanted to bring him along, but it would have been wrong to take him out of school."

"He's a fine-looking boy, if that's what he looks like, ma'am."

"It is. I assure you. I have done him many times before, since he was an infant. Don't you think he has aristocratic features? His father was either my lover, Gambetta, General Boulanger, or Victor Hugo himself."

Longarm didn't know how to answer that, so he didn't even try. Jarret finished what he'd been writing and got up to hand it to Madame Sarah. She took it, read it over, and nodded before passing it on to Longarm. "Monsieur Jarret told me about the tragedy. The young American girl who was murdered while I was on stage. This will be presented to the newspapers at our next stop. Do you think it will help at all?"

Longarm read the press release. It was a generous whopper. According to Madame Sarah, her understudy, the well known American actress, Penelope Wayne, had been killed defending the stage door against intruders during the performance of *Camille* in Cheyenne. Longarm swallowed and handed the note back, saying, "That was mighty neighborly of you, ma'am. Like I told Mr. Jarret, here, the poor little thing was a stagestruck kid from a Kansas farm. It may comfort her folk some to hear she made it into the limelight before getting blowed away."

"*Oui,* I, too, was once a—how you say?—stagestruck kid. But do you know her home address, Custis, *mon cher?*"

"Yep, there were letters from home in her carpetbag. The Cheyenne coroner's contacting them to see if they can afford to ship her body, and—"

"*Mais non!*" the Divine Sarah cut in. "I will not hear of her poor peasant family bearing such expense as well as such grief! You must give Monsieur Jarret her home address. As a member of my troupe, she shall be sent home in a proper casket at my expense."

She turned to Jarret and asked, "How long shall we say she was with us, *mon cher Edouard?*"

Jarret replied, "Since she just arrived from Denver... Perhaps a week?"

"*Oui.* I distinctly remember wiring her contract to Denver, now that you remind me of it. You must send her family her paycheck and compose a personal letter of condolence from me, now that we know where to send it."

Jarret smiled at Longarm and said, "I *told* you she needed money. She's always making gestures like this. I've given up trying to stop her."

Sarah Bernhardt went back to work on the clay bust, saying, "Poof! one does what one can. The world is so cruel, and the child was a fellow artist, *non?*"

Longarm nodded soberly. It was hard to believe he'd ever thought the little gal was sort of homely. Of course, he hadn't known, at first, that she was an angel.

Another pretty gal in a maid's uniform and apron came in from the kitchen to announce something in French. Sarah Bernhardt brightened. "Oh, come with me, *mon cher* Custis," she trilled. "You have never seen me cook. Cooking is my *true* vocation!"

He got up, tossing his hat aside, to follow her and the maid up to the kitchen compartment. He noticed that Jarret and Madame Guerard didn't. They'd likely seen her cook before.

In the kitchen compartment, a pot of onion soup was simmering on the stove. It filled the little room with delicious fumes and reminded Longarm that he'd forgotten to eat supper. It smelled just right to him. But little Madame Sarah gravely removed a red-hot poker from the fire box and dunked it into the soup, saying, "Voila! *Now* it should be fit to serve!"

Then she turned around and marched back to join the others as the cook shot Longarm a weary smile. He said he would carry it, and the French gal thanked him in English. He asked softly, "Does she always do that?"

The cook nodded. "Madame insists on giving each meal her personal touch. It seems to do no harm."

"Can she cook at all?"

"I do not know, Monsieur. She calls what she just did cooking. I never heard of mulling onion soup with hot iron, but, as I said, it does not affect the flavor much."

They took the soup out to the salon and everyone sat

down while the cook, who turned out to be called Mademoiselle Mimi, ladled it out into silver bowls and served toast all around to go with it. Longarm noticed the others dunking the toast in the soup and eating it, so he commenced to do the same and it tasted great. Mimi went back and brought out some coffee and pastry for dessert. Then she sat down and dug in like one of the family. The Divine Sarah called out in her clear voice and another gal in maid's duds came in from somewhere up forward to join them. Her name was Yvette and she was as pretty as Mimi, but different. Mimi was brunette and Yvette was a carrot top. They both filled out their black uniforms nicely. The two French maids were modest-sized, as women went, but Madame Sarah could have fit twice into either of their uniforms. It was hard to see why, since she was eating like a logger. Her table manners were no better, either. Madame Sarah ate the way she did everything else—with gusto. He noticed that she sucked her fingers clean after dunking. But, somehow, on her it looked refined.

The pastries were too sticky and sweet for Longarm's taste, but after filling up on soup and toast he drank a lot of coffee, knowing he had to stay awake despite it's having been a long day. The coffee was strong but tasted funny, like the coffee in New Orleans. They'd told him, there, that it was French coffee, but he'd taken that with a grain of salt up till now. He'd suspected they put all that chicory in it to save on the coffee beans. But Madame Sarah seemed to travel first class, so he figured the French must like their coffee adulterated with weeds. It was strong enough to keep him going, though. He told Mimi he meant to post himself on the rear platform and asked her if she'd leave a pot on the stove for him through the night. She said she'd see to it.

Madame Sarah wasn't paying any attention, but Jarret asked why. So Longarm explained the plan about going over the pass, wording it gently so as not to spook the ladies. Jarret asked what time they'd most likely run into anything. Longarm said, "Depends on what we do or don't run into.

74

If we pull out of here a little after midnight, express, we'll hit the spooky country past Bitter Creek just before sunrise. Owlhoots are sort of unpredictable, though. So I'd best be set as we leave Cheyenne. Are you up to patroling the corridor with your Webley?"

"I am, now. I have a couple of tough stagehands I can arm, too."

Sarah Bernhardt had eaten enough to pay more attention by now. She looked concerned. "Is there anything I can do? I am *très formidable* with a sword. Don't laugh! Because of my figure, I often play male parts for the *Comédie Française*. As the knight, Peleas, in Maeterlinck's play, I was required to brandish a sword, and so I took fencing lessons at the academy."

Jarret laughed. "She's good, too. Don't ever cross swords with Madame Sarah!" Then he smiled at her and said, "I doubt we'll have any sword fights, my dear. I think the best thing for you and the other ladies to do would be to stay well out of the way. Don't you agree, Longarm?"

Longarm nodded. "Everybody knows this is Madame Sarah's private car. Someone made some serious moves against her earlier this evening. So can I offer some serious suggestions, Madame Sarah?"

"But of course, *mon cher* Custis. What is it you wish?"

"Well, until we know if that rascal Brennen shot was the whole show or not, I don't think you ought to bed down here in this car tonight. Ain't there someplace else you could sleep?"

"All the other compartments are filled with my actors and help."

Jarret said, "You could sleep in my bunk, Madame Sarah."

She laughed. "Why, *Edouard*, this is so sudden!"

He flushed and said, "I'll be prowling the corridors like the ghost of the tower, you silly!"

Sarah Bernhardt fluttered her lashes and murmured, "Oh, what a pity. But, very well, I shall—how you say?—hide out in the office car tonight."

She turned to Yvette and spoke in rapid-fire French.

75

Yvette nodded and got up to change the linens, or whatever. As the redhead left, they felt a bump. Longarm managed not to spill his coffee. He said, "That's the cross-country U.P. picking us up, a mite early. I hate to break this party up, folks, but we seem to be off for Utah—and we'd best be on our toes."

Nothing happened for a spell as the special left Cheyenne. Longarm wasn't expecting anything to happen until everyone was bedded down and the train was rolling fast and noisily through Granite Canyon. They were hooked behind an express, so they wouldn't stop often. But even highball trains stopped at places like Laramie, Rawlins, and such.

They were between Buford and Tie Siding, two jerkwater towns they wouldn't stop for, when the forward door of Sarah Bernhardt's car slid open slowly and stealthily and a dark figure entered. The car was dark, but the moon was shining in the windows to gleam on the eighteen-inch bowie in the intruder's right hand as he slid open the door of Madame Sarah's compartment. The same moonlight shone on the empty bed. The man in the doorway cursed under his breath. Longarm's voice was louder, albeit conversational, as he said from the darkness of the curtained kitchen. "I've been expecting you, old son. Drop that knife and grab for the ceiling!"

The would-be murderer dropped the knife, but he went for the gun at his side as he whirled on Longarm with a wild curse. Longarm shot him down.

Somewhere a gal screamed as the man he'd gunned slid down the mahogany with a groan, both hands clutched to his gut. Longarm observed laconicaly, "That was dumb, Brennen. Couldn't you see I had the drop on you?"

The gunshot Brennen gasped, "You was supposed to be out back on the platform, damn you!"

Longarm dropped to one knee, covering the wounded man as he relieved him of his pistol and patted him down for more. All he got for his effort was a palm full of blood. He wiped it on Brennen's coat and stood up to strike a

76

match and light the corridor lamp. "I lied. But that was fair," he told the wounded man. "You lied to me the minute we met this afternoon. You ain't no railroad dick, Brennen. I had that figured even before I got around to reading the wire I got from the U.P. in answer to the one I sent them earlier. You knew that the real U.P. dicks would go on with this afternoon's train, since a deputy marshal was arriving to take charge of this combo. So when I approached you, you told me a fib. I thought at first you were just stupid, but you kept saying you didn't know things a real U.P. dick would have known. You said a yard worker you didn't know told you about the killing. What railroad dick would let a man he didn't know pass him on to railroad property, for God's sake? You knew about the killing 'cause you was *there*—with that other son of a bitch we've got up front in the baggage car!"

"You're loco! I shot him my ownself! He was throwing down on you from behind and—"

"Oh, shit, Brennen, I just shot you creeping into the lady's quarters with a knife in your hand and you're *still* telling fibs! I know you shot your partner, but you didn't do it to save me. You did it to save *you*. You spied him overtaking me on the path. You knew he didn't know who I was, but that I'd likely question him when he come galloping up to you, and you weren't done here yet. So, since he'd already failed at the auditorium anyway, you blew him away to shut him up and to get in better with me."

Brennen moaned and said something awful about Longarm's mother.

Longarm chuckled and asked, "Don't you want to know how I knew he was the one who shot Miss Penny, you poor gutshot bastard! Well, I'll tell you. Your own shotgun hadn't been fired. You made a point of showing it to me. A point an innocent man wouldn't have thought to make. You two planted the bomb in the auditorium earlier today. You likely rode the same train up from Denver and got ahead of me while I was otherwise occupied. You came over here to see if you could worm your way in, just in case, and you did

77

right good, 'cause I was giving you rope from the start, sucker.

"Meanwhile, your pard was covering the auditorium, and we *know* what happened *there*. You'd been out of contact. So when he came puppy-dogging to join you, we know what happened *then*, too!

"But what are we jawing about, Brennen? What I want from you now is some answers to things I don't already know. Who sent you after Madame Sarah, and how come?"

Brennen groaned and rolled over onto his side, vomiting blood. The door slid open at the end of the car and Edward Jarret came in, gun out and leveled. He lowered it when he saw Longarm standing over Brennen, and gasped, "What happened? I was up at the far end when I heard the shot."

"You heard me. I guess this rascal got past you from the tender by crawling across the car tops and dropping down between this car and the next. He was fixing to tell me who sent him after Madame Sarah. Ain't that right, you son of a bitch?"

Brennen didn't answer. Jarret said, "I say, he doesn't seem to be breathing, Longarm!"

Longarm knelt to feel Brennen's pulse and muttered, "When you're right you're right. I must have cut his fool aorta with my round, damn it!"

Another door slid open up the corridor and Mimi stuck her head out. "Get back inside, ma'am," Longarm said. "It's over, and we'll clean it up."

The French gal put her knuckles to her mouth and ducked back inside to slam her door shut, hard. Longarm knew she shared the compartment with redheaded Yvette, so he didn't have to worry about explaining to both. It was likely Yvette who'd screamed when the gun went off. Not speaking English, the maid likely found the West a mite confusing.

Jarret said he'd get some hands to carry the cadaver forward. Longarm shook his head. "He's oozing too much. Why track up the whole special with blood when we can roll him off in a few minutes at Laramie? The sheriff there's a pal of mine and he'll take care of the paper chores. We may as well get rid of the other one, up forward, at the same time. Now that we've got 'em both, I see no need to carry 'em all the way to Utah, do you?"

"You're the lawman, Longarm. But you said before—"

"I know what I said before. I was funning Brennen, here. We were playing dumb at each other and, as you see, in the end he wound up dumbest."

"I do see. But we still don't know who sent them after Sarah!"

Longarm knelt, relieved the corpse of its wallet, and held it up to the light. He took out a card and mused, "This one's from Denver, too. Brennen might or might not have been his real name. But him and that other rascal were signed up as Democrats. When we get to Laramie I'll wire the names and numbers to my boss, Marshal Vail, and let him work on it at that end. Old Billy has friends at the Democratic Club and he's a fair tracker. If these two had known associates in Denver, they're already in trouble."

Chapter 7

After the special left Laramie Longarm found a mop in the
kitchen compartment and cleaned up the mess on the deck.
He had told Jarret not to disturb Madame Sarah, up in the
office car, since she was bedded down safe and likely asleep
besides. Jarret agreed and said he'd find somewhere to flop,
when and if Longarm said it was safe. Longarm allowed
that they were likely out of the woods for now. "If there
was a plot afoot to stop the train in the mountains," he
remarked, "those rascals wouldn't have been out to kill her
aboard her special after failing in Cheyenne. But, if I were
you, I'd flop full-dressed with my gun handy. I'll stay here
in Madame Sarah's car for now."

Jarret nodded, then said, "I say! We do have an extra
compartment I'd forgotten about. The man from the French
embassy got off in Omaha."

"There you go. You take his bunk tonight, and I'll hunker
down here. We'll get things sorted out in Ogden, Lord
willing and the creeks don't rise."

Jarret laughed. "We seem to be playing musical bunks.
But I must say that confuses things for would-be assassins."

He left. Longarm wasn't about to confuse anybody by
flopping in Sarah Bernhardt's bunk. It would be impolite,

81

for one thing. For another, Jarret had a point. Anyone snip-
ing at the special would be aiming at the window of the
petite star who was supposed to be there.

But there were all sorts of places to sit out in the main
salon. He opened the rear drapes for a clear view down the
moonlit tracks through the locked glass doors. Wyoming
was sort of tedious to watch in the moonlight, and they
were going way too fast for a horse to catch now. So he
went up to the kitchen to pour himself some more chicory
coffee.

As he got by the door behind which the two French maids
slept, he heard someone awake. Awake and having a sobbing fit, from the sound of it.

He remembered that they'd never explained what in thunder was going on to the poor little gals and they were likely
still hysterical. He rapped gently on the door panel. Nobody
answered, but the sobbing sounds were heartbreaking, so
he slid the door open with a reassuring smile.

The brunette Mimi and redheaded Yvette weren't crying.
They were going at it in the moonlight, naked as jaybirds
and slurping away as they pleasured one another, contrary
to the laws of Wyoming Territory, with their sassy tongues!
Longarm gulped and quickly slid the door shut, hoping they
hadn't seen him. What they'd been doing wasn't a federal
offense, so he didn't consider it any of his business.

He got his coffee, took it out to the main salon, and sat
down to sip it, staring down the tracks behind them with a
forbidden vision of naked moonlit flesh blurring his view
of the receding ties. The dark one had been on top, and she
surely had a fine little rump. He told the tingle in his britches
to behave. He knew some gals fancied things that way,
unfair as it might seem.

A soft voice behind him said, "Oh, we are so ashamed,
Monsieur. Won't you let me explain?"

He turned his head. It was Mimi, the brunette cook,
wrapped in a sheet and staring wide-eyed at him as she
dropped to her knees near his easy chair. He smiled at her.
"You don't owe me no explaining, Miss Mimi. It was me

82

as was in the wrong. I knocked, but when nobody answered, I acted the fool."

"*Quelle horreur!* Yvette was right—you did see all! I was hoping she was wrong, but..."

"She had the best view of the door, ma'am. But never mind what I might or might not have seen. I don't gossip. Your secret's safe with me."

"Secret? *Mon Dieu!* Do you take us for lesbians?"

"Well, I'd be a liar if I said I'd caught you at bestiality or arson. Let's not fuss about what I call it, Mimi. I told you I wasn't going to say nothing about it to nobody."

"I am not a lesbian!" she pouted. "I know it might have looked like that to you just now. But I assure you, Yvette and I both have male lovers back in France. But we have been away so long, and one must be practical, *non?* Would you have us playing with ourselves?"

"I reckon not. They say that's wicked, too. Look, could we drop the subject, Mimi? I told you it was your own business, and it ain't proper for us to go on jawing about it."

It was making him horny, too, but he never said so. Mimi got up, sobbed, and cried, "This is not just!" as she pattered out on her bare feet.

Longarm muttered, "That's for damned sure!" He sipped his coffee and tried to ignore the full erection that had sneaked up on him while he was talking to a lady who was wearing nothing but a sheet. He had a practical suggestion or two of his own to offer, but he wasn't sure French folk followed West-by-God-Virginia customs in such matters.

They did. The two gals came back, walking hand in hand, both stark naked. Mimi explained, "Yvette does not speak English, but she wants to prove that she is not a lesbian."

Longarm set the coffee aside and got to his feet. The redhead wrapped her white arms around him in the moonlight and started pressing her fuzzy red apron against his fly, commenting in French on what she felt through the rough material down there. Mimi said, "I wish to prove I am not a lesbian, too! She says you are built *très formidable!*"

Well, he didn't want them to take him for a sissy, but the salon was a mite public. So he picked Yvette up and headed for their compartment.

Mimi brought up the rear, pleading, "You will save some for *me, non?*"

Longarm placed Yvette on the rumpled sheets and commenced undressing as Mimi shut and barred the door. The little compartment already reeked of she-male passion, but the gals must have been telling the truth about only pleasuring themselves because they had no men about. For, when he mounted Yvette, she hugged him close and moaned like a lovesick mountain lioness as she commenced to wriggle like a sidewinder under him. Mimi climbed on the bed with them and started beating on Longarm's bouncing rump with her little fists. "Hurry! Hurry! I can't wait for my turn!" she begged.

He did his best. He came fast in Yvette, as any man would have. But she wouldn't let him go and, since he could tell by her contractions she was getting there, he stayed in the saddle to be polite. Mimi wailed, "That is not just! I need it as badly as she does!"

She made a suggestion to Yvette, who laughed and unwrapped her legs to let Longarm withdraw. He saw Mimi on her hands and knees beside them. So he mounted her from behind, and damned if she wasn't built even tighter than the redhead.

He grabbed a hip bone in each palm and commenced to hump her over the Great Divide as she sobbed with joy. Yvette slid under her up front. As the redhead lay back against the headboard, grinning, Longarm saw what Mimi had said to get her to relinquish her turn. For, as Longarm pleasured Mimi right with his plunging maleness, Mimi pleasured Yvette's freshly screwed crotch with her stabbing she-male tongue.

It looked as wild and wicked as it felt. Yvette was grinning at him over Mimi's head in her lap and probably talking dirty, if he could have understood half of it. She said something to Mimi and the brunette laughed, with her mouth full, and twisted off Longarm's stroking shaft to lie face up, sobbing, "Put it in me this way!"

He figured she wanted to finish old-fashioned. But, before he could kiss her, Yvette sat on Mimi's face, facing Longarm, and tugged his head and shoulder up to where he could kiss her, which he did with considerable enjoyment.

The sassy redhead kissed dirty, and Longarm knew he ought to be ashamed of his fool self for letting her wicked mouth defile his pure lips. But somehow he didn't mind. What the hell, it wasn't as if either one of 'em had been doing naughty things with their lips to another man. Leastways, not recently, to hear them tell, and to feel the way they moved.

Mimi came under them. Yvette and Longarm came too—together, sort of. It sure felt funny to have one gal coming in his arms while he was exploding in another. They'd somehow wound up lying sideways with Mimi pleasuring them both. He stopped moving for a spell to get his second wind, and the next thing he knew Mimi was kissing him and rubbing her naked breasts against his heaving chest while he was sliding in and out of one or the other of them. He slid his hand down Mimi's belly until his knuckles encountered Yvette's chin. Yeah, he'd *thought* that might be Yvette he was in now. They were equally marvelous between the thighs. But now that he was getting to know them, he noticed that they contracted tightest on different parts of his shaft.

After a while, even the two hard-up French gals had to stop for a breather. As he lay between them with a redhead snuggled on one shoulder and a brunette on the other, Mimi murmured, "Yvette wants me to tell you she really enjoys *la zig zig* with you. You will not tell Madame about this adventure?"

"Hell, no. But would she fire you if she found out?"

"We don't know. Perhaps not. She is a woman of passion, too."

"Hold it right there, Mimi. I don't want to hear any gossip about your boss lady, hear?"

"Pooh, that is not what we are concerned about, *mon cher*. Yvette and I agree that if Madame ever found out how grand you are where it counts, she might try to steal you away from us. The three of us must be *très* discreet, *non?*"

He muttered, "That's for damned sure," relieved to know that the coming dawn might not be as cold and gray and filled with recriminations as he might well deserve. "After we sort things out in Ogden, I'll be fixed up with my own private compartment," he went on. "I don't reckon we should try her here, once Madame Sarah's bedded down next door."

Mimi said, *"Oui.* She has sharp ears. One of us will always have to stay here, in case Madame rings for service in the night. That means, from now on, only one of us can make *la zig zig* with you at a time."

"I'll try to be a good sport about it. But wait a cotton-picking minute! I forgot all about that Madame Guerard, the one who acts so quiet. Did she go forward with Madame Sarah, before?"

"Mais non. Her compartment is just up the corridor—why?"

"Why? We've been rutting like pigs in a wallow, and what if Madame Guerard heard us? I didn't know she was even aboard this car!"

Mimi began to stroke his flaccid shaft. She soothed. "The old widow always goes to sleep early. And, besides, she never says anything to anyone. They say that is the reason Madame Sarah keeps her as a companion. Madame Guerard is *très* discreet."

He frowned. "She'd have to be, if she hasn't turned the two of you in by now. Come to think on it, she never cracked her door when I had that shootout, and Jarret heard it clean up at the other end of the combination. That's why I forgot all about her. What are you doing down there, girl?"

Mimi didn't answer. She couldn't. She had her mouth full. Yvette rolled over, half on top of Longarm, and commenced to feed him her nipple. He tried, this time, to keep the noise down. But if the old widow woman didn't know what was going on in here by now, she was likely deaf as a post. So the fat was in the fire, and he might as well enjoy it.

Sunrise found Longarm seated innocently on the observation platform with his Winchester across his knees, a cheroot between his teeth, and a weary expression on his face as he rested his butt in one of the big wicker armchairs out there. He'd left the two French maids screwed groggy and, they said, eternally grateful. He was already starting to hate his fool self. He didn't know when he would get a wink of sleep. For a man who hadn't been aboard a horse for a good three days or more, he was as saddle sore as a trail rider at the end of a long day's drive.

But the cool, thin mountain air was bracing, even though it didn't look as though the train was clickety-clacking anywhere near a mountain. The South Pass country was sneaky that way. To north and south, the continental divide rose rawboned in snow-covered granite peaks. But the South Pass was an area where, for some reason, the bones hadn't busted through the prairie sod as the land heaved up. So, while they were still way up in the sky, they seemed to be passing through rolling prairie, just a mite more rugged than the real thing at lower altitudes to east and west. The surrounding swells and draws were ninety percent grass-covered, with here and there a dry wash lined with trees and brush. Only a sharp-eyed Westerner might notice that the trees and brush were mountain aspen and scrub cedar instead of cottonwoods and cherry-bush of the true high plains to the east. Either way, the landscape afforded more cover than a casual glance revealed and, as George Armstrong Custer had found out the hard way, a surprising amount of Indians could be tucked in one of those innocent-looking folds in the tawny shortgrass sod.

But they were on the downgrade and going lickety-split. Nobody on a mortal pony was about to overtake this platform unless they started their run from uphill and cover, closer to the right of way. Longarm wished they'd hurry up and get to the more treacherous country of the Green River Valley so he could wake up.

By another geographic paradox, the trackside country got more mountain-like as they dropped lower on the west slope of the divide, and a man on guard had to look a heap sharper passing through the busted-up aspen ridges west of Bitter Creek.

They'd be passing the jerkwater town of Bitter Creek any hour now. They wouldn't stop, of course. The hour's run between Bitter Creek and the county seat of Green River, where they would have to stop for the mail, was downgrade. One of the first things that had made him suspect Brennen was that the so-called railroading expert had called the roadbed wrong. Longarm knew that if he was out to board a moving train he'd be staked out on the far side of Green River, where the engines had to haul upslope through trees and rocks in a series of cuts and hairpin curves. But some train robbers were dumber than Longarm, so he knew there'd be enough worry to keep him on the prod and awake once they tore through Bitter Creek and hit the timber, even moving fast.

The door behind him opened and a familiar elfin voice said, "Ah, here you are, Custis *mon cher!* Don't you ever sleep?"

As Sarah Bernhardt took the other seat, Longarm smiled at her. "Not on the job, ma'am. You're up mighty early, ain't you?"

"*Oui,* I am too excited to sleep late in a strange bed, even alone. *Edouard* just told me how you saved my life last night. I do not know what to say!"

"Shucks, ma'am. I never saved anyone's life. You were nowhere near when that idjet slid open the door on an empty bunk."

"Brrr! I *would* have been, had not you devised your *très amusant* game of musical beds. Do you think the danger has passed, Custis?"

He turned to reassure her and noticed for the first time that her kimono was sort of open. Her little tits were right firm and yummy for a gal in her mid-thirties who'd mothered at least one child. He looked away and said, "We don't have to worry about Brennen and Smith no more. I hope to learn by wire in Ogden if they were part of some Know-Nothing plot, or just loco on their own. Ah—ain't you cold out here, ma'am?"

"*Mais non,* your Western air is *très* refreshing, and I have always felt too warm at the temperature most people prefer. My doctors tell me my delicate lung condition, while hopefully arrested, causes me to run a chronic low-grade fever. I wish women were not required to wear so many clothes, don't you?"

He chuckled. "I might design skirts a mite shorter if it was up to me. We'll never live to see it, though. They make too much money covering you ladies from chin to toe in expensive cloth. I suspicion us men are allowed to dress more sensible 'cause denim and even broadcloth run so cheap that a yard or so lost don't matter."

"*Oui,* I am sure the designers hate women. When I was younger, women were allowed to show more of their arms and décolletage, but then they insisted on enveloping our lower limbs in so much crinoline we could barely walk. Now that the hoop skirt is passé and one can get by with only one petticoat at a time, the monsters have decreed that we must cover our shoulders and throats with horrid, stiff bodices. There is no justice!"

A cluster of frame buildings and a windmill-fed water tower suddenly whipped over their shoulders and started receding down the tracks behind them. She brightened and asked, "Oh, what was that?"

"Bitter Creek, ma'am. We're making good time. Last time I passed through here on this same run, I was having breakfast in the dining car."

"*Oui.* I shall be cooking our breakfast in a little while. Mimi is beginning to prepare things for me to cook. I think the poor child is suffering from *mal de* elevation this morning. When I awoke the girls just now, she seemed *très fatiguée.*"

"Well, mountain air affects some folks like that, ma'am."

"Not me. I feel filled with energy this morning. Your Western country is so beautiful, and I am beginning to love the people out here, too! I am still—how you say?—Yippee! after being treated so kindly last night in Cheyenne. After the way I was treated back East, I was afraid your Western desperados might hang me from a tree!"

"We only do that to horse thieves, ma'am. Cheyenne felt Yippee about you, too. I reckon you made 'em feel sort of cultured, and ever'body likes to feel cultured."

"I still face your mysterious Utah Mormons with dread. Is it true they do not approve of wine with dinner, *mon cher?*"

"They don't allow smoking or coffee, neither. But don't worry about it. Ogden's a railroad town with lots of gentiles like you and me working there. The elders are tolerant of bad habits as long as the gentiles respect theirs."

"Ah, *mais non. You* are a gentile, Custis. As your New York newspapers never tired of reminding me, I am considered a Jewess, here."

"Maybe. You're still a gentile when you get to Utah. I've noticed other Jewish folk find that amusing, too. But, to the Latter-Day Saints, all outsiders are gentiles, even Chinamen and Shoshone."

She laughed her meadowlark laugh. "How droll! I have been called many things, but never before a *gentile!* Do you think these Mormons will enjoy *La Dame aux camélias* as much as the nice people in Cheyenne?"

"I hadn't studied on it till just now. I ain't sure *Camille*'s the play for a Mormon audience, ma'am. You see, the Saints is sort of proper. And old Camille's sort of a—well, sort of French."

"Oh, *mon Dieu!* What am I to do, then? We have already booked the theater in Ogden, and even as we journey there tickets are being sold for tonight's performance!"

He took a thoughtful drag on his cheroot. "Well, really stuffy Saints ain't likely to buy tickets in any case and, like I said, there are lots of gentiles there. Why don't you just go ahead and put on any old play you're comfortable with?"

She sighed. "My very favorite role is *Phèdre*. My company knows it, since I perform it often in France. *Edouard* Jarret told me it might be too—how you say?—highbrow for American audiences. *Phèdre* is a Greek tragedy, you see."

"Spoke in Greek, ma'am?"

"Silly! In French, of course. I love the role, but *Edouard* says it would be over the heads of Americans, even in English."

Longarm said, "I ain't no expert on show business, but I reckon I know Americans out here as well as anybody, ma'am. I suspicion a highbrow play they couldn't half understand might seem cultured as all get-out to the folk in Ogden, and nobody who don't want to be cultured is likely to buy a ticket to see you in any case. The Mormons set great store by education. There's hardly a Mormon kid in the Great Basin as ain't forced to go to school right through the spring plowing. They say the Book of Mormon was written in Egyptian, originally, and the elders all claim vast education no matter what they raise for market. I suspicion a Greek tragedy would sure hit the spot with them bearded old elders and their womenfolk."

She clapped her hands. "We have all day to rehearse, too! Oh, Custis *mon cher,* how I wish we'd known you in New York! The critics were so cruel! I wept and I wanted to go home. But *Edouard* said they might like me better out here, and now I see that he was right!"

She rose lightly to her little feet and took Longarm's free hand. "Come—Mimi must have started breakfast now, and you must be *très* famished, *non?*"

He leaned the Winchester against the chair and got up to follow her inside. He saw that Edward Jarret and Madame Guerard were already sitting in the salon, waiting for the Divine Sarah to stick a hot poker into whatever Mimi was making for breakfast.

Jarret had dark circles under his eyes, which was only reasonable for a man his age who'd been on guard all night. The handsome Madame Guerard sat secretive as Mona Lisa and relaxed as a contented house cat. When Longarm greeted her, the widow woman just nodded and met his eyes, calm and friendly. She didn't look as though she knew what he'd been up to with the maids, just around the bend from her own compartment. But, on the other hand, when Mimi came in to announce breakfast was ready to be "cooked," the sassy little brunette looked like butter wouldn't melt in her mouth. As the Divine Sarah followed her to the kitchen, Longarm noticed that Mimi walked as if she were a mite saddle sore, too. But that was the only indication she gave that she'd been at all improper in the wee small hours.

Jarret said the servants had fixed up the vacant compartment for Longarm in the car ahead. "From the looks of you, I'm not the only one who could use a few winks, Longarm. How soon do you think it will be safe for us to kip out?"

Longarm said, "San Francisco, mayhaps. But, since it ain't possible to go that long without sleep, I figure to catch forty winks once we're past the Church Buttes, about an hour west of Green River. If nobody smokes up this special by then, they ain't seriously studying to. Too many settled spreads along the trackside, beyond the buttes, for gents to ride mysterious."

"That's good to hear. How far is it to Ogden from Church Buttes?"

"Couple of hours or so. It'll still be early morning when we roll into the Ogden yards. While we wait for the town to wake up, you and me can get some sleep up forward."

Jarret said, "You can, perhaps. I have to arrange for the show this evening, challenge at least one local newspaper man to a duel, and in general make sure Ogden knows we're there. There's no reason why you couldn't sleep until afternoon, of course."

"Yes, there is. I got some telegraphing and investigating chores. So you won't find me in bed at high noon! I have to pay a courtesy call on the local law and check out the theater for any dismal surprises."

"Won't you be too tired to keep an eye on things tonight,

when we may really need you?"

"I'll be bushed, but not that bushed. I don't need much sleep. If I catch an hour or so this morning and maybe kip out for a siesta this afternoon between my law chores and the show, I'll make it."

Yvette came in ahead of Mimi, with the Divine Sarah bringing up the rear. The two maids got to tote the grub on trays, of course. Sarah had likely finished "cooking" the scrambled eggs with her poker and let the hired help do the hard parts.

Yvette looked innocent as hell, too, considering. Longarm was starting to feel better about his moments of weakness in the maids' compartment. Yvette didn't even walk as though she'd been screwed silly. He'd noticed she was built stronger in the legs than Mimi.

Aside from the eggs, which came from hens instead of fish after all, there were fancy rolls and all the chicory coffee one could drink. He drank at least a quart with his breakfast before he was done, for two reasons. He was heavy-lidded, and the eggs tasted sort of weird.

He already knew that French folk put all sorts of herbs in their coffee, but it was surprising to find mushrooms and chopped-up onion-grass mixed into his scrambled eggs. He was too polite to comment on Madame Sarah's culinary notions. So, when she asked him how he liked his "omelette," he was slick enough to remember that was what some fancy folk called scrambled eggs and allowed he liked his omelette fine. Madame Guerard was looking at him with amusement as he washed each bite down with coffee. He wished she'd talk more. A gal with eyes that knowing could spook a man when she never came right out and said what she was thinking.

They'd just about demolished breakfast when the train stopped at Green River. Longarm was as surprised as the others when he heard a brass band outside playing the French national anthem. Jarret laughed. "I say, there seems to be a crowd out there, Sarah. I think you'd better step out on the platform and say a few words to them, what?"

"In my kimono? How long shall we be stopping here, Custis? Is there time for me to dress and put on some makeup?"

"No, ma'am, and they'll be disappointed if they don't even get a wave from you. They must have read in the papers you'd be passing through Green River, and they don't get much culture out this way."

The Divine Sarah stood up. "I can't! I won't! My hair is a mess!" But, as Jarret opened the door to the observation platform for her, Sarah Bernhardt took a deep breath, threw back her shoulders, and stepped out into the morning sunlight to face what looked like a German band surrounded by a lynch mob.

As Longarm and Jarret followed her out, Longarm could see that more folk than could possibly reside in Green River had ridden in off the surrounding range to have a look at a real French actress. Sarah blew them all a kiss and the crowd went wild. Cowhands threw their hats in the air and a fool in the rear ranks emptied his sixgun into the sky as a delegation dressed in their Sunday best pressed forward, packing flowers and another wooden key to the city. Longarm turned to tell Jarret they'd best make sure the engine didn't start as soon as it was finished taking on water. But he saw that the Englishman had already thought of that and had gone forward.

The Green River town leaders lined up across the tracks behind the platform, and one held up a little gal holding a mess of fresh-picked mountain flowers. As the child held them nervously out to the Divine Sarah, the Frenchwoman took child and all in her surprisingly strong arms and swung the kid aboard the platform, standing her on one of the wicker chairs as she kissed her. That hit the crowd as right neighborly, and they started roaring even louder. Longarm moved his Winchester out of the way so the kid wouldn't shoot herself in the leg. The little girl was confused but smiled up shyly as Sarah Bernhardt stood beside her with an arm around her shoulders and held up her other hand for silence. Longarm saw that the gent with the big wooden key was confused, too, so he reached over and took it. The gent shot him a relieved grin. Longarm wondered who they thought he was.

As soon as she could be heard, Sarah Bernhardt said, "I am overwhelmed by this great honor, mesdames and messieurs! I wish there was more time for me to stay in your great city—but, alas, we are already running late."

A cowhand on a jaded pinto called out, "Aw, hell! I rode nigh twenty mile to see you do your stuff, little lady! Cain't you show us a sample of your acting at least?"

The Divine Sarah smiled radiantly and began to recite her poem about the two lovesick pigeons in French. The crowd fell silent, awed by her magic voice. Longarm found it awesome, too, as he watched this bitty, no-longer-young, skinny woman, with her fizzled hair a mess and not a speck of powder on her big, shiny nose, carry a posse of hard-cased mountain folk over the rainbow to fairyland with her magic voice and her winning ways.

Most of them would have been content to hear the pigeon poem, not understanding a word of it. But there was one spoilsport in the crowd and, as she finished with a flourish, he yelled out, "Aw, hell! Don't you know nothing in American, gal?"

Others shushed him, of course. But Madame Sarah called out, "Forgive me, monsieur, you are right!" Then she raised her hand in a soldierly salute to the flag over the little brass band. And then, in a voice that filled the valley with goose bumps, Sarah Bernhardt began to recite Lincoln's Gettysburg Address. Not even Sarah Bernhardt's voice could be heard above the thunderous roar of approval and joyful pistol shots. But she went right on reciting, hugging the little Green River gal with one arm and saluting with the other. The train suddenly started moving. Longarm grabbed the little gal and swung her down into the arms of her dad. Sarah held the salute as the train pulled out of the station with everybody waving and cheering her. But as they rounded a bend she suddenly sank down in one of the chairs and covered her face with her hands, sobbing fit to bust.

Longarm placed a gentle hand on her heaving shoulder. "You've no call to weep, ma'am. I'd say if you ever ran for mayor of Green River, you'd *win!*"

She looked up at him, tears running down her cheeks, and said, "It was such a cheap, theatrical trick. Patriotism is the last refuge of a passé actress. There was a time when I did not have to resort to the obvious, Custis. There was a time—I know you will not believe me—when I was really great!"

"Oh, hell, ma'am, you're great right now. I 'fess you brought a lump to my throat, too, back there. You're about the greatest actress I've ever seen, and that's no bull."

She took his hand, kissed the back of it, sisterly, and said, "You are, as ever, gallant. But I feel the magic slipping through my fingers, Custis. We live such mayfly lives, and our numbered days run so swiftly through the hourglass. How long will I have it? How long will I be able to hold them in the palm of my hand, as I did just now? I am already old for an actress. In a few short years I shall become a pathetic shadow of what I am today. I have sworn suicide before I have to fall back on the devices of aging actresses. But I am weak. I shall probably never kill myself, even when I have to stage jewel robberies and last appearances to get my name in the papers."

"You're a long ways from retirement, ma'am. I'll likely be retired from the Justice Department and even married up and settled down long before you take your final curtain call."

"*Oui*, I won't have the sense to retire, as long as I can totter out on the stage. But even if we both live into the next century, Custis, *le bon Dieu* just does not give us enough *time!*"

The gloomy discussion was interrupted, to Longarm's relief, when Jarret came out to join them. He took in the situation at a glance and said, "I say, I want you rested for tonight's performance, dear girl. You know *Phèdre* takes a lot out of you, even when you're up to snuff. If you insist on putting on your epic for the desert rats ahead, *I* must insist that you get more rest. Are we likely to be met by any more brass bands in the near future, Longarm?"

"Not hardly. I'll sit out here till we pass the Church Buttes and make sure nothing else unexpected happens. You go along with Ed, Miss Sarah. He's right about you looking tired."

Jarret said he'd told Yvette to show Longarm to his new quarters when he was ready for a nap. Then they left him alone to contemplate the passing scenery as the train wound upgrade through gray boulders and green barked aspen groves.

Chapter 8

The wine-fresh mountain air, the strong coffee, and the possible dangers from trackside kept Longarm awake until, off to the near horizon, he saw the Church Buttes, which looked just like what they were named after.

He stood up and stretched as a couple of longhorns stared at him over a trackside snow fence. The train passed a homestead with a sunflower windmill spinning merrily in the morning breeze. He stepped inside and found Yvette seated in the salon, darning socks. She brightened and got to her feet, babbling at him in French. He knew that Jarret had ordered her to lay in wait and see him to his quarters, so he just followed her without trying to figure out what she was saying. As they passed the doors of the sleeping cubbyholes, he saw that they were all shut. He hoped the high-strung Madame Sarah was taking her manager's advice to catch a few more winks.

Yvette led him along the corridor of the car beyond and pushed open a compartment door. As Longarm stepped in, she followed and shut it behind them, locking the latch. The compartment was small but luxurious. Yvette or someone else had already made up the wide bunk and turned the covers down for him. The crisp linen sheets looked very inviting. Then he saw that Yvette was peeling off her prim maid's uniform.

He said, "Hold on, gal! It's broad daylight and I'm tired besides!" But she didn't savvy English—and, whatever Yvette was, she wasn't all that tired. He shrugged, put his rifle in the corner, hung his hat on a hook over his frock coat, and unbuckled his gun rig. "Well, if you're taking off *your* duds, I may as well do the same," he said.

Yvette beat him into bed, naked save for her black cotton stockings and high-buttons. She had had less to take off in the first place, and seemed more eager to shuck. He forgot how tired he felt as he saw the way the sun coming through the windows played on her red hair. But he knew they were acting dumb, and if he'd been able to communicate with her better, he'd have told her so.

They communicated in another way as soon as he climbed into bed with her. It turned out better than he'd expected. Either Yvette was a mite tuckered, too, or she was content to do it more romantically now that she had no other gal to compete with. He entered her like they were old bed pards and she just took him on old-fashioned, kissing sweetly and moving her rump sassily.

No man born of mortal woman could have failed to get an erection looking at such a pretty redhead in the altogether. But, between fatigue and the showing off the night before, Longarm could only post in the saddle, not really trying to get anywhere soon. From the way Yvette crooned and kissed him, he could tell she liked it that way, too. She wrapped her strong thighs around his waist and contracted in orgasm at least three times before he got there. And when his own mounting desire made him move faster in her, she hissed with passion, dug her nails into his back, and they came together in a long, sweet, shuddering moment.

As he lay in her arms, Longarm sighed and said, "I hope you won't think I'm a sissy, honey, but . . ."

She shushed him with a finger against his lips, shoved him gently out of her saddle, and said something about "discreet," which anyone with a lick of sense could follow.

Yvette sat up and slipped her duds on faster than seemed possible. He lay smiling up at her fondly and trying to keep his eyes open to be polite. The redhead kissed her finger, pressed it to his lips and his flaccid tool, and leaped up to let herself out. Longarm struggled up, locked the door, and flopped face down to sleep the sleep of the unjust. He got almost two full hours before the dirty son of a bitch driving the engine pulled into Ogden and he had to get up again.

At the Western Union Office near the Ogden depot, Longarm found no messages from his home office. That figured. Billy Vail would be up and about in Denver right now, but it could take some time for even an old Texas Ranger to find out anything important about Brennen and Smith, if those had been their real names. Meanwhile, Billy Vail was not a man to waste the taxpayers' money on wires that didn't say anything.

The Ogden papers carried the tale of the murder in Cheyenne the night before. It was sort of nice to read that the late Penelope Wayne had been a promising actress in the Bernhardt company and Madame Sarah's chosen understudy, and that her killers had been brought to justice. It wasn't going to do Penny any good, but at least she'd be remembered as famous in her tiny Kansas town.

The headlines didn't exactly hurt Madame Sarah's future ticket sales either, he imagined. But he didn't think she'd made the decent gesture for that reason. So he got mad as hell when he read what one fool put on the cultural page about Madame Sarah's daddy being a rabbi and her mamma a notorious French actress, too. At least they hadn't spelled it "rabbit," but they had everything else wrong.

Ogden was a railroad town set in the middle of nowhere important. Mountains rose beautifully to the east, but everything else was covered with soot and powdered, dry horseshit. The sun was getting up there and the wind off the Great Salt Lake just steamed things up without really cooling or wetting down the dust.

He went to the local U.S. marshal's office to check in

and possibly get some temporary local help. The marshal was off hunting rascals who'd been selling firewater to the Utes. His office clerk seemed to have come out of the same barrel as prissy Henry, back in Denver, but he wasn't as nice as old Henry.

The bastard said they hadn't been asked for assistance by Washington and that Longarm and Denver were on their own. Longarm told him he was a mule-headed fool and left.

He had better luck with the town law. The Ogden police seemed flattered to be asked to help guard the national treasure of France. The chief said that he and his missus had already planned to attend the play that evening, and that he'd be proud to provide uniforms at all the entrances and exits. Longarm shook on it and didn't ask for any detectives. He figured he could check out the theater for explosives and such as well as anyone. The Ogden law agreed to meet him at the theater an hour before it opened that evening. While he had the chief in such a good mood, Longarm asked if there'd been any outbreaks of Jew-baiting in Ogden of late.

The chief frowned, thought for a moment, and shook his head. "Nothing serious," he said. "I disremember there being enough Jews in Ogden to bait. When the boys get surly they generally chase a Chinaman, and they hardly do that no more, now that the rails are all laid around here. Why? Are you Jewish?"

"No. Miss Sarah Bernhardt is—sort of. She's been getting hate mail from Jew-baiters, and the gents who gunned her understudy last night, thinking she was the star, seemed to hate Jews past common sense."

The chief looked surprised. "Well, I never! Wait till I tell my missus we're going to see one of the children of Israel as well as an actress tonight! Being Mormons, we takes the lost tribes of Israel serious. Brother Joseph Smith wrote a lot about 'em. Some say the Injuns is one of the lost tribes. But, with all due respect, I've always took that with a grain of salt. We'd sure like to meet up with a child

102

of Israel in the flesh. Do you reckon you could introduce us to her, Longarm?"

"Sure. Hang about after the show and I'll fix it up for you."

"Lord, wait till I tell my Vinnie! What's Miss Sarah really like, Longarm? We've heard so many different things."

"She's a great lady—and a nice little gal, besides. Don't worry, Chief. Your wife will get along with her fine. I'll see you all later, at the theater, hear?"

He left the police station to prowl further. The Mormon chief's openminded attitude didn't surprise him much, but he knew that Ogden was only about a quarter Mormon. Folks who worked and drifted with the rails came from all over, from China to Constantinople. So one could meet up with damned near anything in this tawdry little town.

He saw the three gilt balls of a pawnshop up ahead and remembered the gent who ran the operation, for they'd had discussions about stolen property in the past. But since fencing for local burglars and pickpockets didn't come under federal law, he passed on by. The one-eyed Irishman who ran the place likely wouldn't tell him if there were any serious owlhoots in town, even if he knew.

He saw a familiar figure up on the boardwalk ahead and slowed. It was Mimi. The brunette had changed from her maid's uniform to a print summer dress, but there was no mistaking that rump and that walk. He didn't want to catch up with her. He knew it was her turn, and he was busy with more important business. So he lagged behind until Mimi turned into a doorway. Then he went on by, walking fast. She was likely shopping or something. But it sure was odd that she'd turned into a door with a red lantern over it.

He stopped a kid on the next corner and asked, "Say, pard, is that frame house back there the kind of house I think it might be?"

The kid grinned. "It is if you think it's a whorehouse. Best one in town. But they ain't open this early."

Longarm thanked the kid and walked on, frowning. He supposed it was possible that Mimi worked on the side during layovers, but it sure didn't match up with the tale she'd told about being hard up, with a lover back in France.

The mystery was explained when he turned into a saloon to get out of the sun for a spell and wet his whistle. He spied Latour, the Divine Sarah's butler, drinking alone at the bar. Longarm bellied up beside him and said, "Howdy, Latour. How do you like American beer so far?"

The little Frenchman sighed. "It has an admirable presumption. I do not usually drink this early, but I have just had a most fatiguing argument with that silly girl Mimi, and I need something to calm my annoyance."

Longarm signalled for a drink and asked Latour what he and Mimi had been fussing about.

"She wished to quit," Latour said. "Can you imagine such a thing? She insists that she means to desert us, out here in the middle of the great American desert!"

"She may have heard that this is a land of opportunity. Did she give you any reason? She seemed happy enough this morning."

Latour shrugged. "She says she is afraid she'll be murdered next. She began right after she read this morning's newspapers. I told Madame it was a mistake to engage bilingual servants. She says that last night the full import of all that was going on had not been clear. Now that the papers are hinting at a plot against Madame's life, Mimi says she would rather starve than go on with us."

"She won't starve," Longarm muttered into his beer schooner. He didn't tell Latour why. Mimi had treated him right, and it was her own business if she chose to get paid for what she did so well for free.

Latour finished his beer and refused another from Longarm, saying he had to find an employment agency, if they had one in Ogden. So they parted friendly. Longarm decided to settle for one drink at one place at a time, since he had many places to cover. He didn't envy Latour. He and the butler had a lot in common. They were both looking for needles in a haystack. Latour had to find another French gal who could cook and maid—in Ogden, Utah—while

Longarm had to see if he recognized any faces as he prowled about.

Like most lawmen worth their salt, Longarm carried an awesome mental rogues' gallery of faces in his memory. Nobody could remember everybody, so when he was looking for bank robbers he dredged up bank-robbing faces to look for. Right now he was trying to remember political agitators and secret-society lunatics he'd brushed up with in the past. But all he found in the next three saloons were plain old Utah boys.

It was getting to high noon, and if he meant to go on nursing beers and eyeing strangers from under the brim of his hat, it was time he considered packing away some grub. Madame Sarah's mushrooms and scrambled eggs hadn't stuck to his ribs worth a damn. He remembered a fair diner, over by the railyards, where locals in the know went for lots of decent grub, cheap. It was off the main drag and you had to know your way. It was likely cheap because they didn't advertise.

He almost missed it, even knowing it was there, by heading down the wrong side street. Then, as he saw the yards and parked railroad cars ahead, he got his bearings and walked down to where the place was tucked between a coal tipple and a lumberyard. Nobody ate there but railroad workers and smart hobo gents with change to spare.

He went in and saw that he'd beaten the noonday rush. So he took a seat at the counter and asked the Greek behind it for some of his famous roast beef and hash browns, with real Arbuckle coffee, even if he had to pay extra.

The Greek growled that they never served nothing but Arbuckle, damn it. And sure enough, they did; it tasted like honest trail-camp coffee, strong enough to stand the spoon up in.

The roast beef and hash browns were the way Longarm liked them, too, cooked nice and greasy in salt sowbelly shortening with plenty of catsup over them.

He finished the main course and allowed he'd have some of their fine apple pie. By now the Greek could see he was a good old boy, so he cut the pie extra wide and filled his coffee mug another time without being asked. Longarm chuckled. He'd feared that by now this place would be famous and overcrowded, but he was almost finished with his pie before another customer came in, hot and dusty.

Longarm had just heard a train whistle, so he figured the newcomer had just dropped off it passing through freight and, like anyone who knew Ogden, knew the best place near the yards to eat.

The stranger started to take a seat down the counter, shot Longarm a curious look, and went for the gun on his right hip.

It didn't work. The stranger had telegraphed his killing intent with his eyes before slapping leather. So his muzzle was still in his holster as Longarm beat him to the draw and jackknifed him around a .44 round in his belly. The stranger's own gun went off, still half holstered, blowing leather as well as gunsmoke into the floorboards while Longarm parted the man's hair, through the crown of his hat, with a second round. He thudded to the floor and just lay there.

Longarm told the frozen-faced counterman, "It's all right, I'm law. Do you know who that poor bastard might have been?"

"I think I've seen him in here before. Not recent. Maybe six or eight months back."

"There you go. Like me, he remembered how good you brew Arbuckle, and we both got lucky. Lock the door a minute, will you? I want to pat him down. It makes me nervous to have folk busting in on me as I'm concentrating."

The Greek moved around to the front, pulled down the curtain, and shot the door bolt as Longarm went through the dead man's pockets. He found a personal calling card made out to someone named Brown. The only other thing in his pockets was a couple of sets of playing cards—marked. The easiest way to tell a marked deck was to riffle them while looking at the backs. The backs of honest cards formed a more or less steady image as they flickered. The extra dots on a marked deck made a little dancing pattern.

Longarm felt the forearms of the corpse and, sure enough, there was another deck clipped to his left forearm, under the sleeve.

Longarm straightened up. "Well, I hear voiced objections to your closing so early, out front. We'd best open up and explain Mr. Brown to all interested parties."

The Greek opened the door. An Odgen copper stepped through it first, gun drawn. Longarm had holstered his own and the copper knew him from the police station earlier that morning, so it went all right. The copper said he'd see that the cadaver was sent over to the coroner, and, since it had been shot proper, there was no reason to pester the poor Greek about being a witness, save for the copper's own report. Longarm told the Greek he was sorry and left an extra dollar on the counter before he stepped outside.

There were others gathered, of course. Longarm spied Edward Jarret in the crown and hailed him. Jarret joined him, saying, "I might have known it was you I heard from the train just now. What happened?"

Longarm told the Englishman about it as they strode across the yards together. "Haven't you any idea who he might have been?" Jarret asked.

Longarm said, "No. It happens that way sometimes. If he was on my wanted list, I'd have recognized him sooner. As it was, things got sort of tense back there. He was a drifting gambling man with a guilty conscience. That's all I know for sure right now. I shot another gambling man in Denver the other night, and the mysterious Brown might have been his pard. On the other hand, he could have just done something serious, recognized me as a lawman, and panicked. We'll know better if and when we learn if anything serious has taken place within a day's freight ride."

As they approached the special on its siding, Longarm noticed that nobody was staring out the windows, despite the recent shots. When he commented on it, Jarret said that Madame Sarah and her actors were over at the theater, rehearsing the new play they meant to put on.

Longarm said, "Damn it, Ed, you shouldn't have let her

go till I scouted that fool theater."

Jarret shrugged. "You must know by now that nobody tells Sarah Bernhardt what she can or cannot do. Don't worry. I'm not that stupid. I told my stagehands to search high and low for suspicious packages and to bar and guard the doors. The men who work there regularly will help, and they'd naturally notice if anything looked unusual back stage, right?"

"I reckon. Have you sent the scenery over yet?"

"No. Sarah wants to get the feel of the theater without the stage set. You see, sometimes a bothersome echo can be mended by reshifting the stage props, and—"

"I follow your drift," Longarm cut in. "One of us should hang about here at the train till Latour, at least, gets back. You want to flip for it?"

"I have to run over to the theater in a few minutes. Tickets and all that. But what danger do you foresee here at the train, Longarm?"

"Bombs can be taped under a train as easily as under a stage. You run on to the theater and I'll see if I can scout up some railroad bulls to make sure nobody skulks about who don't belong."

That reminded him of something he'd been meaning to ask. "Could you put me some numbers on the troupe, Ed? I notice you and Madame Sarah don't socialize all that much with your inferiors."

Jarret said, "It's not a matter of social inferiority, old boy. Sarah carries democracy to self-destructive lengths at times, by picking up the damnedest stray cats. The star of a theatrical company maintains a professional distance from her supporting cast because it's—well—professional."

"You mean like officers and enlisted men in the cavalry?"

"Exactly. You can't give unpleasant orders to a person on one occasion and pal about with them on another. Sarah directs as well as acts in her plays, and despite her casual attitude about most things, she's a very serious actress and a bloody terror about setting up a scene. We're short one male support because he missed his cue in Omaha."

"She fired somebody in Omaha?"

"She did indeed. That's one of the reasons the man from the French embassy left us there, too. It seems that the lad had political connections in France. His name was Sardou, Jacques Sardou. His uncle is an important playwright, and another one is a member of the National Assembly. We brought him along as a spear carrier, hoping that, at the least, he wouldn't trip over the scenery. But he did, and he missed cue after cue besides. Sarah might have forgiven him if the audience had been kinder to her in Omaha. But, since they hissed her, exit Monsieur Sardou. Dumont, the man from the embassy, went back with him to make sure he made his boat, and doubtless to suck up to his outraged uncles."

Longarm shrugged and said, "Well, since he's gone, he ain't acting too suspicious. I still need some educated numbers to go with who might or might not belong on that train section."

Jarret nodded and began to reel off names. "Let's see, there's the orchestra and stagehands and some of their wives or mistresses. I'd have to consult my list. I can't name them all from memory."

"Give me a round number, then."

"Say about thirty, give or take a lover's spat. The cast on stage consists of Sarah, of course, and her present supporting cast of seven. Three female and four male."

"Do tell? I could swear I saw more folk than that on stage with her last night. Course, I was watching the audience, and I never counted."

"Eight on stage can look like the population of Verona if they know their trade," Jarret replied. "The human eye only counts to three before most people have to move their lips. Anyone can tell the difference between a pair or three of anything without counting. But once you have four or more milling about..."

"Don't tell your granny how to suck eggs," Longarm cut in. "I'm a lawman. Witnesses can't tell if it was four or five men who rode off after a holdup. So I see how it works

109

on stage. When you get a chance, I'd like a written down roster of everyone in the troupe. I ain't about to memorize all them French names by ear alone. For now, just tell me who's the he-star and the runner-up she-star to Madame Sarah."

Jarret shook his head and said, "I can't. They don't exist. You see, Sarah rotates the parts, both to give the actors experience and—well, frankly, to keep anyone but herself from being vital to the tour. Leading men have a habit of falling in love with their leading ladies, and any actor or actress who gets too many favorable reviews has a tedious habit of demanding a raise or indulging in temper tantrums about billing."

"You mean, if I were one of Madame Sarah's actors I'd likely carry a spear one night and get to kiss her the next?"

Jarret chuckled. "That's about the size of it. As a matter of fact, the male lead tonight will be played by a soubrette, Mademoiselle Laval. Phèdre is an older woman who lusts for a much younger man, you see, and so little Claudette Laval will be her intended victim."

Longarm frowned thoughtfully and said, "I should have let her stick with Camille, with Saints in the audience. Is this here Phèdre a *dirty* play?"

"I'd say it was more a matter of forbidden passion. Don't worry. Obviously, neither lady can take off her clothes in the love scenes. I have to go, Longarm. Meet you at the theater."

Longarm nodded and Jarret lit out. Longarm strolled the length of the combination, circled, and headed back down, checking under the cars between the trunks for anything Pullman hadn't put there as original running gear. As he got back near the observation platform, a burly gent with a burly pit-bull dog was coming up the tracks. They recognized one another on sight.

"Howdy, Dutch," Longarm said. "Is that dog as mean as you?"

"Nobody's mean as me, but he'll do," the yard bull said. "I just heard that some lawman shot a hobo over to the Greek's. Was that you?"

"Yeah. Lucky for you, I seen him first. He dropped off a freight with a Harrington Richardson .45 on his hip."

Dutch opened his denim jacket, exposing the walnut grips of the gun he carried in a shoulder rig. "Oh, I wouldn't say that. I'm sorry he got across my yards, Longarm. That don't happen often."

"I know. He seems to have known the Ogden yards. How many boys do you have under you today, Dutch?"

"Three men and this dog. Why? You expecting more trouble?"

"Not if you and your railroad bulls are keeping an eye peeled."

He went on to fill in the tough but genial Dutch on the possible dangers to the troupe and its combination.

Dutch said, "Hell, you go on about your business and let me worry about folks putting infernal devices betwixt the trucks. We can't be ever'where at once. That's how come that hobo you shot got off that freight alive. But knowing this varnish combo is special, I'll make sure nobody skulks about it."

Longarm thanked the yard bull and climbed aboard the platform. Now that the coffee and the excitement at the Greek's was wearing off, he realized that the little sleep he'd caught that morning wasn't going to carry him through the evening bright-eyed and bushy-tailed after all. He looked at his watch and saw he could steal four hours before he headed for the theater. If he showed up about five, he'd have a good three hours to look under every seat in the blasted place before the curtain went up that night.

Chapter 9

Longarm let himself into the salon, where he found Madame Guerard sniffing along the baseboard on her hands and knees, like a hound dog looking for a place to pee. He couldn't help noticing that, for a gal who must be at least fifty, she had a tolerable rear end.

He said, "Ma'am?" and the Frenchwoman rose to her knees, blushing and flustered. "Oh, it is you," she said. "Forgive my appearance, I am *très distrait*."

"You look upset, too. Lose something, ma'am?"

Madame Guerard brushed a strand of silver-dusted black hair from her forehead and sighed. "I search for the Tear of Dumas. I can't find it anywhere."

"That's one of Madame Sarah's jewels, ain't it?"

"Oui, her favorite, and the only really valuable piece she still owns. It is a formidable diamond, cut in the shape of a tear, on a silver chain. Alexandre Dumas *fils* gave it to her years ago after she appeared in one of his plays. She is most sentimental about it, but Madame is so careless with her things."

"I noticed you sort of have to pick up after her. Did you say that diamond was one of her *only* valuable jewels, ma'am? Seems to me she's got a heap of play-pretties."

The Frenchwoman looked away. "That is true. I didn't know what I was saying," she murmured.

He smiled down at her gently and said, "Sure you did. The others are mostly fake, ain't they?"

"Whatever are you saying?"

"I won't tell if you won't tell, ma'am. It just stands to reason a gal who owes part of France's war debts to Swiss bankers would have converted her jewelry to cash and paste by now. How long have you been missing her last real diamond?"

Madame Guerard leaped to her feet and grabbed his sleeve, sobbing, "You must never breathe a word of your suspicions, even to Madame! She is so proud, and so delicate. My petite Sarah is not well, Monsieur."

"Simmer down, ma'am. I'm a lawman, not a tattletale. Let's us concentrate on the real diamond some more. You were fixing to tell me when she first missed it."

"Mon Dieu! She does not know it is missing! That is why I must find it! I was just, as you say, picking up after her, when I noticed the Tear of Dumas was not in its usual place in her jewel box."

"Could she have worn it over to the theater?"

"Mais non—I dressed her myself. At the moment she is wearing a rather ordinary choker of, ah, pearls."

"Yeah, I've seen them pearls they make out of herring scales. You're right, nobody can tell unless they test 'em with their teeth. Have you looked under all the seat cushions?"

"Alas, I have looked everywhere more than once. The diamond is just not here!"

"How 'bout up forward, in the other cars?"

"Mais non, Madame never goes forward, and..." They grinned at each other as they both remembered the same thing at the same time. Madame Guerard said, "But of course! She slept last night in Monsieur Jarret's compartment!"

He followed her forward, but when they got to the door of Longarm's compartment, he said, "You go on and pros-

114

pect for diamonds, ma'am. I'm about to fall on my face. Could you fix it so somebody wakes me up before five. I can't trust myself to wake up that sudden. For I've messed up the alarm clock in my brain by mistreating it some of late."

She said she'd wake him herself and headed on up to Jarret's office car. Longarm left the door unlatched so she could. It was againt his principles, but with the car deserted inside and old Dutch and his dog patrolling outside in the hot sun, it seemed safe enough.

Longarm stripped, got into the bunk, and fell asleep right off. So the next thing he knew he was dreaming a dirty dream.

It seemed he was up on a theater stage with the Divine Sarah. Nobody in the audience seemed to notice he wasn't a real actor, or that he'd somehow wound up out there in the limelight without a stitch on. He was still trying to figure it out when he noticed the Divine Sarah wasn't wearing anything but the Tear of Dumas. He hauled the gal in and planted a kiss on her mouth.

She kissed back, nice, but as they came up for air and he ran his free hand down a surprisingly shapely torso that felt more like silk than skin, she gasped, "Monsieur! Just what are you suggesting?"

That was when he opened his eyes and saw that he had Madame Guerard in the bed with him. She felt silky because she was still wearing her summer frock. He was bare, of course, and since the sheet had been kicked off as they wrestled, he couldn't move away from her without exposing his hard-on. So he didn't. He said, "Howdy, ma'am. I'm sorry—but, you see, I was having a dirty dream."

She lay beside him, putting her own hand down on the wrist between them as she murmured, *"Oui,* that seems obvious." But, instead of removing his hand from her lap, she moved it thoughtfully, and he realized he had her soft mons cupped in his palm through the thin silk of her skirt. She wasn't wearing a petticoat or anything else underneath. He had no idea what a man was supposed to say to an older

115

lady at a time like this, so he kissed her some more, and he could tell from the way she kissed back that he was forgiven.

Being a widow woman as well as French, Madame Guerard had sense enough to haul up her own skirt as he went on petting her. So, as his fingers entered her, he could tell from the way she was lubricating down there that though there might be a little snow on her roof, there was still plenty of coal in her furnace.

As he started to mount her, she said, "Wait, let us be practical! I do not wish to rumple my dress, *mon cher!*"

So he eased off and leaned on one elbow as she sat up and hauled the summer frock off over her head. He was glad she did, for Madame Guerard was built well. As she lay back down beside him, he could see that while time had been sort of ornery to her still handsome face and turned the hair between her thighs snow-white, those thighs and the body they packed around were so smooth and shapely that a gal of twenty might well envy her.

He rolled atop her, kissing her and meaning to mount. But she kept her legs down together and rolled her lips from his to say, "One moment. You must promise me one thing, Custis *mon cher.*"

"Honey, you can have the moon and the stars if you'll just relax some."

"I wish nothing for myself. It is Madame I am pleading for."

"Thunderation! You want to play three-in-a-bed with Sarah Bernhardt?"

"Such a thing is unthinkable! I know what you did with those naughty girls last night. I see now why they wanted you to. But if I give myself to you, you must promise not to make improper advances to *ma petite* Madame! Is it agreed?"

Since he'd been ordered, direct, by Billy Vail, and hadn't been invited by the Divine Sarah in any case, Longarm said, "We got a deal."

Madame Guerard sighed, spread her thighs, and, as he

entered her, gasped, *"Mon Dieu!* I think I just saved the life of my employer! You might have warned me!"

But, for a gal who seemed to think she was sacrificing herself to save her boss, old Madame Guerard sure seemed to enjoy it as they commenced to pleasure each other. Longarm found that there was something to be said for older women with still-youthful figures.

Being experienced as well as well built and likely lonely, Madame Guerard moved like an old familiar song as she played his thrusting shaft like a flute. He ejaculated sooner than he wanted to, but any man would have with such a partner.

And it was easy to keep going. The old French gal was doing more than half the work as she held his chest against her soft breasts and drummed the heels of her high-buttons on his bounding butt. She didn't tell him when she was coming. There was no need to. He was glad she made love quietly. He might have known she would. Mona Lisa smilers were like that. A man hardly ever got caught with shy gals who smiled like Mona Lisa in mixed company.

He wanted to do it some more, but she said, "Not now. You just came again with me. I felt it. You must get dressed and go to the theater, you naughty boy."

He stopped moving, but remained in the saddle, enjoying the way she pulsated. "You're right, damn it," he said. "By the way, did you ever find that diamond?"

"Non, and I don't know how long I can keep it from Madame."

"Hell, honey, you'd best tell her soon. The loss has to be reported to the law. Local law, that is. Jewel thieving ain't federal, so I can't put out a federal flier on the loss. I'll tell the Ogden police chief, and since he's a fan of Madame Sarah—"

"Sacre bleu! You must not, Custis! I forbid it! Madame has to put on a most exacting performance this evening, and you know she already suffers from stage fright. If she had even more to worry about—"

"I savvy. We won't tell her. Hey, you sure are tight."

117

"What are you doing? I thought we were going to stop. You must stop, Custis *mon cher*. It is after five, and ... Oh, don't stop. Don't *ever* stop!"

It wasn't until Longarm was fully dressed and halfway over to the main street that he realized he still didn't know Madame Guerard's first name. He smiled crookedly and decided it didn't matter. He surely wasn't going to ask her now. She seemed to like "honey" well enough in bed, and she'd warned him they had to remain "madame" and "monsieur" in company, even if she did creep forward to join him later tonight. There was much to be said for this French discretion. Though some of the bedroom farces they put on were starting to make more sense, lately. Madame Guerard knew he'd been discreet with the redhead, Yvette, already. So he figured he'd let the gals work out the details. He didn't see how he could lose, and he liked surprises.

He got to the doorway with the red lantern over it and went on in. A professor wearing sleeve garters on his striped shirt and a tough expression on his face intercepted Longarm in the dark hallway and asked, "Do I know you, friend?"

Longarm said, "Not hardly. I ain't a customer. I'm the law—federal. I know you have the local law paid off, but since that's none of my business we'll say no more about it. Are we dealing friendly, or do I have to bother with search warrants, grand juries, and such?"

"Hey, take it easy, marshal! There's no need for you and me to have us a war! This is a respectable house. Ask any married man in Ogden. Who are you looking for, some federal want knowed to enjoy feminine charms?"

"Nope. A French gal with charms of her own to spare. She just went to work for you today. Name's Mimi. Show me to her crib and I never saw this place. Deal?"

"You got it. I told the madam she looked like she was on the run. Follow me up the stairs and I'll lead you to her direct. What's she wanted for?"

"That's up to her. Just show me her door and go have a drink or something."

The man led him along a domino row of identical doors,

pointed out one with his chin, and said, "She's all yourn."
Longarm turned the knob and went in.

Mimi was sitting on a cot in her shift, with mirrors on
three walls reflecting them both. She blanched when she
saw who he was.

He nodded to her. "Yeah, I figured it out, Mimi. If you
just hand it over, we'll say no more about it and you can
go on with your more honest trade. Otherwise . . . well, I
can see you're a gal who thinks fast, so you don't want the
otherwise, right?"

"Custis *mon cher,* whatever are you talking about? I am
très confused and embarrassed to be caught in such a place
by you. I was hoping nobody would ever know, but a girl
must live, and I was discharged without enough money to
get home to Paris, so . . ."

"I ain't got time for bullshit," he cut in. "I'm already
overdue at the theater. Let me spell it out, so you'll see I'm
smarter than you took me for. You've been planning from
the first to steal the Tear of Dumas. Since you knew the
one real diamond from all the paste, you have to be an
experienced jewel thief. You must have been sore as hell
when you found out after taking the job that most of Madame
Sarah's famous jewels are junk. But anyone with an eye
for diamonds can spot the real thing when it sparkles in
candlelight."

"I don't know what you are talking about."

"Sure you do. You couldn't steal it when Yvette was
about. The redhead's naughty, but not a thief, or you'd have
lifted the stone together long before this. Most nights Madame Sarah's locked in with her jewels. Since they bedded
you with Yvette, and next to Madame Guerard, you ain't
had much opportunity to prowl solo. You seduced Yvette
to get in good with her, but you hadn't converted her to
stealing yet. Last night you meant to pleasure her to sleep
and creep into Madame Sarah's empty compartment. That
would-be murderer, and my horny nature, foiled you. But
things were still all mixed up at daybreak. Jarret, your boss
lady, and Madame Guerard were all back in the salon after
breakfast, with you two gals forward. Yvette took me to

my own quarters, bless her. That's when you had the chance to slip into Madame Sarah's compartment, right across from the kitchen, and snatch the diamond. The rest we know. You quit in a made-up huff and came here to sign on as a whore. Not because you needed the money, but because you figured it was the last place a gent like Latour would look for you once the Tear of Dumas was missed."

He chuckled. "You forgot that I wasn't such a gent as Latour. So let's get to the bottom line. You've got the diamond somewhere in this crib, for I just checked with the only fence in town and he never heard of you. The question before the house is whether I have to tear this crib apart and arrest you when I find it, or if you want to save me some time and yourself a heap of trouble. What's your answer, girl?"

"Custis, you would not put poor me in jail, after all we've been to each other?"

"Not if you hand it over right now. I'm a sentimental cuss that way."

She started to cry.

Longarm said, "That won't work, and I don't want to screw you again, either. I'm in a hurry, Mimi. Give me the damn diamond and we'll say no more about it."

"I have your word?"

"*Oui, oui.* But make it snappy. Like I said, it's getting late."

Mimi sighed, rolled off the bed, and bent to pry up a floorboard, exposing her naked rump, probably on purpose. But he just stood there, calmly looming, until she produced a waxed-paper package and handed it up to him with a sad little sigh. "How am I to ever get back to Paris now?" she wailed. "I was counting on selling that for my passage home."

He opened the packet, saw the cold fire of a real diamond, and slipped it into his vest pocket with his watch. "You'd have made more than passage home, I'd say. But don't worry about money, gal. They say this is the best whorehouse in town. Have you served anyone yet?"

120

"Oui," she pouted, sitting back on the bed. "And I don't think I like this business much."

"Hell, Mimi, you'll get used to it. You have the makings of a natural whore."

For some reason, that made her roll over on her face and commence to blubber. Longarm left the crib, told the worried professor downstairs that he'd made a mistake and the French gal was ready for a customer, then walked on to the pawnshop he'd seen earlier.

The door tinkled as he entered the dark shop. A one-eyed man wearing an eyeshade peeked out from behind some drapes in the back, groaned aloud, and came out to say, "Don't tear the place up this time, Longarm. Tell me what the hell you're looking for and if I've got it I'll produce it. Thief's honor."

Longarm chuckled agreeably and said, "I found what I was after, doc. I lied about you some, gulling a greenhorn jewel thief just now. But we made a deal and it's over. I came to deal with you, too, if you know what's good for you."

The fence looked worried. "I swear I don't know what on earth you're talking about, Longarm. I ain't dealing in any goods Uncle Sam might be interested in."

"That's why I won't arrest you. I want two favors from you, doc. Do you feel like doing me two favors?"

"Within reason. Name your pleasure."

"Well, for one thing, I want you to spread the word that Madame Sarah Bernhardt, whom you must have heard about, is touring the country with a vast collection of fabulous jewelry that's mostly pure glass. So, if any of the pros you deal with try to steal it, they'll be wasting their time as well as ducking my bullets. How fast and how far can you spread that, doc?"

The fence shrugged. "I know you won't believe this, but I don't really know *every* jewel thief in the whole country. Since I know you're a man of your word, I'll see at least some of my—uh—associates get the word. What's the second favor?"

"You and your crooked friends are honest crooks who only thieve for a living. Both lawmen and honest thieves know crazy folk who run about acting ornery just for the hell of it are just needless confusion in an already troubled world, right?"

"No argument. Mad-dog killers and gents who steal she-male unmentionables off clotheslines make it hard for decent crooks. Are you talking about the lunatics who killed that actress gal over in Cheyenne? I read about it in the papers."

"I am, doc. I hope I gunned the two who done it. But they might not have been the only ones. I want you to spread the word along the grapevine that some ornery amateurs might be dogging Sarah Bernhardt's tour. Should any pick-pocket, pimp, jack-roller, or other gent who watches the street for a living notice anything I miss, they're to pass it on to me. In return, the angels will record a modest point on their yellow sheets, and you never know when you might want to ask a friendly prosecution for a reduced sentence or such, right?"

The fence said, "I know how informing works. I'll do what I can. But I can't promise much."

Longarm nodded and turned to leave, with the one-eyed fence following. As they got near the front door, Longarm pointed with his chin at a saddle on a wall hook and observed, "You ought to move that army saddle back out of sight from the street, doc."

"Shit, that's government surplus, Longarm."

"Do tell? Well, it has the same regimental numbers that was reported a few weeks back. Seems some rascals busted into an army depot and helped themselves to a mess of new issue not too far from here. But you wouldn't know about that, would you?"

"Hell, no. We both know I'm an honest pawnbroker. I'll put the word out for you, Longarm. Where are you all headed next, in case you need to look up the local honest crooks?"

"Salt Lake City, I think. But don't worry, doc. I never need help at finding gents in your line of business."

Chapter 10

Madame Guerard was at the theater when Longarm got there. He found her alone in the green room and, when he gave her the diamond, she gave him a kiss, took him by the hand, and led him up to a box overlooking the stage. The audience was empty, the actors on stage were busy practicing, but when Longarm started fondling the French lady she made him stop. So he had to watch the rehearsal.

He couldn't understand word one, of course, but it was sort of interesting just the same. Madame Sarah was seducing the gal who'd be playing a young Greek boy on stage later that evening. Since they were both dressed she-male it looked more scandalous than it would have if young Claudette Laval had been a real gent. Madame Sarah wasn't acting anything like Camille. She'd changed her voice all husky and really sounded like an older, wicked temptress. Claudette was less convincing as a boy, but she sure acted tempted. As they rolled about on a divan, all hot and bothered, Longarm said to the woman at his side, "Uh . . . Madame Sarah ain't—well—like Mimi and Yvette, is she?"

Madame Guerard laughed. "That is one vice I can swear she's never tried, save on stage. On stage, of course, Madame can be anything from the Empress Theodora to a minstrel boy. If the part required her to be a lesbian, she would act the part with gusto. I think she would kiss a crocodile, if the part called for it."

The younger actress, Laval, had given in to temptation and had "his" temptress down, kissing hell out of her, now. It looked really dirty to see two gals in summer smocks carrying on like that. Claudette Laval had a really nice rump and she was wiggling it sassy as she swapped kisses with Madame Sarah. Madame Guerard guessed what he was thinking, just as she could guess which way to move in bed. She was one savvy old gal. *"Mais non,* Mademoiselle Laval is not a lesbian, either. I suspect, before he was sacked in Omaha, that she was sleeping with young Jacques Sardou. That may be why he started missing cues and stumbling about on stage. As you can see, she moves her derrière well, *non?"*

"I sure hope she don't shock the audience tonight. She's shocking hell out of me, and I ain't a Mormon elder!"

Down on the stage, Madame Sarah called a sudden halt to the love scene and got up as if nothing had happened to announce that rehearsal was over and that everyone should eat and get into their costumes. Longarm asked the gal in the box with him if she wanted to mosey over to the Greek's, but she said she had to help Madame get into her Phèdre duds. So they parted friendly.

As the cast and stagehands filed out the stage door to grab some food nearby, Longarm scouted the theater alone, looking for dynamite and not finding any. Somebody pounded on the stage door and when the regular doorman opened up, a squad of Ogden coppers came in to report to Longarm. They'd already eaten, so he showed them where each should post himself during the show. Then, knowing nobody could sneak in while he wasn't looking, Longarm went and filled his own gut. The Greek wasn't sore at him about the shooting that morning. He said it had been good for business, since folks had dropped in all day to hear about it. He gave Longarm some venison he'd set aside for special customers.

Longarm took his time, and got back to the theater early

anyway. He was glad he wasn't an actor. For, while it sounded exciting, life upon the wicked stage was as bad as the army when it came to "Hurry up and wait." It seemed to take longer to set a play up than it did to play the fool thing once the curtain rose. Folks ran about backstage like chickens with their heads cut off, and no matter where Longarm stood, he managed to be in someone's way. A young gent wearing a short Greek tunic and a gilt fireman's helmet bumped into Longarm and would have fallen down had not Longarm grabbed him and said, "Steady, old son." The boy blushed beet-red and stammered in French. French was close enough to the way you said "excuse me" in English for Longarm to savvy. He understood why the French boy was blushing, too, so he let go of her tit and told her he'd meant no harm. She ran off, flustered, and he realized it had been Claudette Laval whom he'd mishandled by accident. Her long bare legs were covered to the knee in those shin plates warriors had worn in the olden times. He reckoned she *could* pass for a warrior now. She'd sure fooled him for a second there.

He went out front to get out of the way and cover the crowd as they started filing in. He spied the police chief and his lady, so he led them up to a box. When Vinnie asked when *Camille* figured to start, he told her, "Any minute, only it's another play tonight. Don't get upset by the love scenes, ma'am. They're just acting, see?"

He left them to move to the rear, where he'd left his rifle with the limelight crew. They looked like they wanted him out of the way too, so he hefted the Winchester and moved to a corner from where he could fire at anyone who started anything anywhere this side of the footlights. He knew Jarret and a couple of Ogden coppers were armed and watching backstage and that the stage door was barred to anything smaller than a battering ram.

The little orchestra started playing spooky, kind of oriental music, and the curtain went up to let the magic begin. Longarm tried to concentrate on the heads seated down there between his muzzle and the Divine Sarah, but it wasn't

125

easy, for damned if she wasn't topping her performance of *Camille* within minutes.

She and the others spoke in French, the play was unfamiliar to American audiences, but they lapped it up like kittens at a milk saucer.

Miss Phèdre wasn't a bit like Miss Camille. He'd thought the night before that Sarah Bernhardt was taking advantage of her own frail frame to play a poor, sick gal wasting away with something awful. But Sarah Bernhardt was just as convincing as a spitfire Greek siren who could chew up men and spit out boys. She looked bigger and stronger, and she moved like a tigress in heat, till every woman in the audience was clutching on to her escort lest Sarah steal him, and every man was sort of wishing he could get stolen.

Nobody cried for Phèdre as they'd cried for poor Camille. Not at first, leastways. But, as the play wore on, the gals in the audience stopped hating her and started feeling for poor, crazy Phédre as a weaker-willed sister they secretly savvied. They could see old Phèdre knew she'd done wrong by lusting after forbidden fruit. So by the last act she was in a hell of a mess screaming to the Greek gods that she was sorry, but that if she had it to do all over again, she'd likely be as ornery.

As the curtain went down, the audience stood up, clapping and yelling fit to bust. Madame Sarah came out to take a bow or a dozen, blowing kisses and catching roses as her big eyes made love to them all. And they all loved her back.

She made her other actors come out and take bows, too. Then they tried to get off the stage, but the audience kept calling and clapping and making the whole cast take one curtain call after another until Jarret came out and said he was sorry, but they had to knock it off.

Longarm let the crowd thin some before he cradled his rifle and went to find the police chief and his wife. He told them to follow him and they acted like kids at the circus when he led them backstage to the green room. Jarret had been warned, so he had a seat and some refreshments set up for them. Claudette Laval, still in costume, poured some

126

wine for them, not knowing they were Mormons.

Vinnie gasped, "Land sakes, are you a girl?" When the pretty French girl allowed that she was, Miss Vinnie was so flustered that she picked up the wine and drank some before she knew what it was.

But she was a good sport and just put the rest down, laughing. Sarah Bernhardt came in wearing her kimono, and all the gents stood up. She came over to the police chief and kissed him on the cheek, bold as brass, to thank him for guarding her life. Then, before Vinnie could say anything, Madame Sarah kissed her too, so the Mormon gal knew it was all meant innocently.

Longarm didn't see any murderers in the green room, so he ducked out. Jarret followed. The big Englishman said, "I think the danger has passed, Longarm. There hasn't been one suspicious incident tonight."

Longarm nodded. "One star don't make a sky, Ed," he cautioned. "How many more of these nights have we to study on?"

"Let's see. Tomorrow we play Salt Lake. Then it's west to Virginia City, Frisco, down to Pueblo de Los Angeles, and back along the southern route to Texas and points east. Where will you be leaving us?"

"Don't know. My office ain't wired me yet. They'll likely call me off in Texas. You'll need deputies who savvy Dixie more'n me, once we hit East Texas. We'll cross that bridge when we get there. I figure—let's see—six or seven more stops, out here in the West. You can get Madame Sarah and the others back to the train safe enough. I got to get to the Western Union before it's time to leave."

"Sure. Wiring your office for further instructions?"

"Nope. Instructing the yard bulls in Salt Lake City. You see, it's only about an hour's run south from here. So, even if that cast party lasts till all hours, we figure to be sitting on the siding in the Salt Lake yards most of the night. Sitting still outside of town. Anyone stalking you folks must know that too. It's the best place between here and Frisco to catch us as sitting ducks."

127

Longarm didn't just wire Salt Lake City to alert the yard bulls that a Pullman special full of innocent lambs didn't fancy being slaughtered in their sleep. He found a wire from Denver waiting for him. As he'd hoped, Marshal Vail had spent the day tracking down the true identities of Smith, Brennen, and Brown. The shabby gambling man he'd gunned that morning could still be anyone, but Billy Vail said that the two gents from Denver were known in some circles not as Know-Nothing fanatics, but as guns for hire. Old Billy had put their descriptions together with the infernal machine and, since few hired guns used time bombs in the first place and the suspects he had in mind had really been named Brennen and Smith in the second, he was damned if he didn't think he had the right ones.

Longarm took the telegram with a grain of salt. He supposed bad guys voted, too, and you had to register to vote. But, on the other hand, someone knowing the name of a hired gun who wanted to be him could just go down and get a card and . . . That wouldn't work, either. Nobody with a lick of sense used the alias of a known hired killer when he was out to kill somebody. Billy could be right. It happened that way sometimes.

But if Brennen and Smith had been hired killers, someone had *hired* 'em! Anyone who had the money to hire once could always hire again. It would save a lot of tedious ducking if he could find out who the spider was in the center of this infernal web.

As he left the Western Union office a reptilian individual wearing a coachman's hat and a Mexican poncho slithered up beside Longarm and said, "They calls me Little Dipper. I'm a friend of One-Eyed Doc. Have you ever heard of a hardcased gent calt the Dorado Kid?"

"I have. It's been said that if he gave his mother a box of chocolates she'd have to watch out for ground glass. Has the Dorado Kid been seen in your fair city, Little Dipper?"

"He has. At the moment, he is lurking in the Hang-dog Saloon, drinking alone and wearing a double-action .44 on each hip. He ain't said who he's looking for tonight, but as he's generally looking for somebody, Doc said you'd want to know."

"I do, and I thank you both, Little Dipper. Since picking pockets ain't a federal crime, don't think this gives you a license to work sloppy. But if you ever get caught with U.S. property on you, drop me a line and I'll see what I can do."

The Little Dipper slithered off into the darkness like a sidewinder as Longarm stopped under a streetlamp to consult his watch. He saw there was still plenty of time, so he headed for the Hang-dog.

When Longarm shoved through the swinging doors, the piano stopped and someone muttered, "Oh-oh!" For word had gotten around that Longarm was in town.

The Dorado Kid was drinking alone down at the far end of the bar. He had that end all to himself. The Dorado Kid had that effect on folk. He wasn't really young enough to be called a kid any more. The Dorado Kid could be five years either side of forty, give or take hard living. He was dressed dusty blackboard from Justin boots to Stetson hat. The border rig he wore his black-gripped Colts in was plain and businesslike. He wore both guns cross-draw, grips forward, like Longarm wore his own. The Kid hadn't gotten the name from being Spanish. His hawklike face was tanned as dark as many an Indian's, but his eyes were the color of raw oysters, and about as friendly, when Longarm bellied up beside him and said, "Evening."

The Dorado Kid said, "I'm drinking alone, friend."

Longarm held up two fingers to the barkeep. "No, you ain't. I can see I have the advantage of you, Kid. They call me Longarm. I'm the law, and we're fixing to share some liquid and information or we're fixing to have an awful fuss. What's it going to be?"

The Kid's eyes narrowed thoughtfully, but his hands stayed on the bar as he considered his options. Finally he said, "I've heard of you. I personally think you're overrated. But wolves hunt sheep, not one another. So I'll drink with you, as long as you understand I ain't *afraid* of you."

"That sounds fair. I ain't afraid of you either."

Longarm waited till the barkeep put two glasses in front of them and crawfished back out of range before he said, picking up his redeye, "I have a lawful reason for being in Ogden tonight, Kid. Would it be too much to ask what you're doing over on this side of the mountains? You generally hunt the high plains, don't you?"

The Kid picked up his own drink and took a sip. "It's a free country, Longarm. A man goes where he wants to."

"Goes where he wants to, or goes where he's *sent,* Kid?"

"Are you accusing me of anything in particular, or are you just fishing?"

"Fishing, *serious,* Kid. You know I'd arrest you if I had anything to accuse you of direct. This sure is rotten bourbon. We could likely save us drinking another if you'd open up some. I'll put my own cards on the bar for you. I ain't interested if you're gunning for somebody local. I'll be leaving soon with an acting troupe I'm guarding. We're headed down the line to Salt Lake City. Will you be following?"

"What if I say yes, Longarm?"

"I strongly advise against it, Kid. I'll tell you true, I don't mind drinking with you, but you make me nervous. There's no telling what I'd do if I ran into you unexpectedly in Salt Lake or points west."

The Kid downed the last of his redeye and held up two fingers as he said, "Don't run into me then. And don't try to buffalo me, Longarm. I ain't scared of you. We both know you can't throw down on me without a reason. So until you has a reason, I reckon I can come and go as I damn well please. You're with that Sarah Bernhardt outfit, right? Tell me something. Is it true she's Jewish?"

"Oh, hell, are you a Know-Nothing as well as a hired gun? I swear I don't know what all the fuss is about. Madame Sarah don't look or act all that different from you and me, save for being she-male and likely a nicer person."

The barkeep replaced their glasses and muttered, "I'd

sure like to close for the night, gents. It's getting sort of late—no offense."

The Dorado Kid ignored him and mused aloud, "So she *is* a Jewess. I'd heard she was."

"Didn't the folks as hired you say so, Kid?"

"Who says anybody hired me, Longarm? What if I was to tell you I was a tourist, looking to gaze on the wonders of the West?"

"Well, I hardly ever call a man wearing two double-actions a liar, Kid. But I must say your words startle me some. I know you've somehow managed never to shoot anybody federal. But since we're old drinking buddies, I feel safe to say you have a certain rep that don't include much innocent sightseeing, or innocent anything else."

The Dorado Kid finished his drink, dropped some coins on the bar, and said, "It's been nice talking to you, Longarm. But, like the man says, he wants to close. I'll see you around."

As he strode for the swinging doors, Longarm growled, "I sure hope not, Kid." But the tall dark killer just went out into the night without looking back.

Longarm saw no need to finish the awful redeye remaining. He put two bits on the mahogany and said, "Keep the change." He headed for the back, but didn't use the gents' room. He ducked out the back door into a pitch-black alley, got his bearings, and headed for the railyards. He didn't think the Dorado Kid was likely laying for him in the dark out front, but things like that could happen.

By the time he got back to the special, the others had beaten him from the theater. So he scouted some, met a yard bull who told him that nobody seemed to be lurking about, and climbed aboard the observation car. He found Jarret, the two Madames, and the butler, Latour, interviewing a new cook-maid he'd recruited in Ogden. She naturally spoke French. After that, it got sort of strange.

The bitty gal Latour had found was from French Indochina, and looked it. She said her name was Lame Duck, as close as Longarm could pronounce it. Madame Sarah pronounced it Lamb Duke, which sounded even dumber. The little Oriental gal kept correcting her till Madame Sarah solved the problem, at least to her own satisfaction, by changing her name to Lulu.

Lulu said she'd come to San Francisco with a French family a spell back and had been stranded when the lady fired her. She said Monsieur had been all right to work for, but that his wife had been a terror. Lulu hadn't liked it in Frisco, she said, because the Oriental gents there were damned old Cantonese in the first place and horny as hell in the second from not having enough China gals to go around. Old Lulu had been working her way back home by cooking or doing laundry, depending. She seemed a mite confused as to which way Indochina was. She was a pretty little thing and spoke French as well as English with a French accent. But she didn't seem too bright. Jarret muttered as much in old Sarah's ear.

Madame Sarah said, "Pooh, the poor child is bewildered, as she has every right to be, *non?* Tell me, Lulu, can you prepare cuisine in the French manner?"

"Mais non, Madame. I learned to cook from *ma mère."*

"No matter. I shall teach you how to make a serviceable vinaigrette in no time at all. She shall sleep with Yvette, Monsieur Latour. You can take her forward and introduce them, *hein?"*

As the butler led the little Oriental gal out, Longarm turned to Jarret and said, "I see you have the shades down. Keep 'em that way. The locomotive will be picking us up in a spell. It's only a short run down to Salt Lake. If you'll sort of keep an eye on things, I'll relieve you in Salt Lake and you can get some sleep."

Jarret nodded and asked, "Are you turning in now, then?"

Longarm shook his head, ignoring the hopeful look in Madame Guerard's eyes. "Nope. There's a local way-freight about to leave ahead of you for Salt Lake. I'm fixing to ride down in the caboose and get there well ahead of you."

The two French gals looked surprised, but Jarret smiled. "Good thinking. Anyone laying in wait for us down the line

132

knows our timetable and expects you to be aboard, eh?"

"Yeah. The yard bulls in Salt Lake have been alerted to look out for prowlers. But they won't look serious till they know your train's coming. I'll get there an hour or so early and see if anyone needs a boost over the fence. Sneaky is a game that any number can play."

Chapter 11

It didn't work. Longarm made all the right moves. But when he beat the Bernhardt special to Salt Lake by over an hour and dropped down off the way-freight, he was met by the boss bull of the yards, who told him they'd asked for extra help from the Salt Lake law and gotten it. Longarm scouted the yards anyway, but all he got for his pains was a mess of dogs barking at him and some yard bulls asking him who the hell he was and what he was doing there.

But at least when the troupe arrived in the wee small hours Longarm knew it was safe to just climb back aboard and get some sleep. He boarded his own car, knowing Madame Sarah and her hired help would be kipped out by now. He met Jarret in the corridor and told the Englishman the war was over for the night, adding, "Nothing bigger than a rat could creep up on us right now—and I wouldn't bet on a rat getting away with it for sure."

Jarret headed for his own quarters and Longarm headed for his own.

Madame Guerard was waiting for him in bed, with even her shoes off, this time. He chuckled, said, "Howdy, Pard," and made sure the door was locked before he undressed and got in the feathers with her.

The sort of old but youthful-natured French gal welcomed him with open arms and thighs. It felt nice to enter her like an old sidekick a man didn't have to shilly-shally with. The only silly thing she said, as they commenced, was that she wanted to thank him properly for recovering the lost diamond. He allowed that this was a fair reward indeed, but he knew damned well she enjoyed it as much as he did—and would have, even if he hadn't gotten the Tear of Dumas back.

After they'd come old-fashioned, Madame Guerard wanted to get on top. In the moonlight through the window, her bobbing breasts looked twenty years old as she posted on his saddlehorn. He had to allow that her fifty or more summers gave her certain advantages.

She moaned and whispered, "Oh, me, too!" as he shot his wad up into her pulsating innards. Then she collapsed atop him and lay still with her soft, warm torso pressed to his and her moist love box sucking him gently.

"I wish I could spend the whole night here with you, *mon cher,*" she murmured. "But I dare not fall asleep in your arms. I must be in my own compartment when Madame awakes—and she rises early, alas."

"Well, I ain't sleepy, and you don't have to leave just yet, do you?"

"Mais non. I am as hot as you, you naughty boy. I confess I do not have as much opportunity for this sort of thing as I did in my younger days. Do you know you are the first man I have made love to in America?"

"Welcome to the States. Don't you have nobody in France?"

"But of course. Nobody sleeps alone in Paris unless she wants to. But things are different here, and in England, where we just toured. You Anglo-Saxons are so strange about *amour.* Why is it that you have a house of ill repute in every town, but look down so on women who enjoy sex, too?"

"I've always wondered about that, too. Don't judge us all by Queen Victoria, honey. Some of us are good sports."

She laughed and started moving her hips, slowly and teasingly, as she said, *"Oui,* that is what I like most about you, Custis *mon cher.* You are so...so natural in bed with a woman. Even in France, so many men are silly. They either swear undying devotion before going home to their wives for the weekend, or else they treat one like an object to be despised. You really *like* women, don't you?"

"Well, sure. If I didn't like 'em, I wouldn't spend so much time with 'em."

"That is not what I meant. All men act passionate when they are making love. You seem to like women as—well, *people.*"

He rolled her over on her back, not taking it out, and took charge of things. "Yeah," he said, "but some people I know don't move fast enough."

So they went crazy for a while and when they came back down from heaven again he noticed that she was crying. He kissed the tears from her cheeks and murmured, "What's wrong, honey? Did I hurt you?"

"Non, you would not know how to hurt a woman, Custis. I weep perhaps for a girl I used to know. Did Monsieur Jarret tell you where I was when Madame found me and took me under her wing?"

"No, and I don't want to hear. Anybody over thirty who ain't been hurt a mite by life likely hasn't lived all that much, honey. When we met up, you were a fine-looking French lady, riding segundo for a famous actress and flattering hell out of me with her friendship. So let's leave it like that, hear?"

"I was a whore, Custis. A used, abused, discarded woman of the streets. I was ready to kill myself when Sarah recognized me as a once young and pretty widow who used to live next door to her."

"I asked you not to dwell on such matters, ma'am."

"I had been kind to her when she was a child. Nothing grand. Only the small favors one does for a lonely young girl just out of school and confused by grotesque surroundings. You see, her mother and aunts were—ah—business-

137

women, who'd packed the child off to a convent to get her out of the way. She was of an age when they could no longer hide what they did for a living. I sometimes had to feed her when they were entertaining guests."

"Damn it, girl. Now you're even talking dirty about your pals. Why the hell do you fool women always want to confess at times like these? I ain't no priest. I'm *screwing* you, in case you don't notice."

She laughed and said, "Why, so you are! I'm sorry. I am so shy I fear I gush when I meet someone I feel comfortable with."

She wasn't moving shy, and she was gushing indeed as she began to respond again to his thrusts. But Longarm knew he'd be about sated once he made it over the hump this time. She was a nice old gal, but he'd been pushing himself of late, and a man needed a rested mind and body to really concentrate on country matters.

They shared a long, shuddering orgasm, kissing friendly. Then they came up for air. "I really must go," she said. "But would you indulge me one last unusual thrill, *mon cher,* if you are not too tired?"

He hesitated before answering. She'd just told him she used to be a streetwalker. But, what the hell, she smelled clean, and he always tried to be a good sport. "Hell, I'll try anything that don't hurt," he said. "What's your pleasure, honey?"

"I want to fall asleep in your arms. Would you let me?"

"That's all? I thought you had some wild French thrill in mind."

"There are thrills and thrills, Custis. It has been a long time since I indulged myself in that one. You see, with most men . . ."

"I follow your drift." He dismounted and rolled over on his back to cuddle her head on his shoulder. She snuggled close and murmured, "Oh, *oui,* this feels so reassuring. But you must wake me in a few minutes. Can I trust you?"

He cupped her closer, with his palm against her tailbone, and told her to let go as he reached out with his free hand for a smoke. By the time he'd fumbled it lit, Madame Guerard was asleep and purring against him. He smoked two cheroots as they lay there in the silent railyard night. Then an owl hooted and he noticed that his own heavy lids had flickered more surprised than they should have. So he snuffed out his smoke and woke her gently, and she got up to dress and leave.

As she stood in the doorway, he asked when she'd be coming back. She sighed and said, "Never, *mon cher.*"

"Never? Never's a long time, honey. Did I do something wrong?"

"You did everything all too *right.* I am afraid I am beginning to fall in love with you, Custis, and a woman in my position must be *très* discreet. I think it better to end it before we get in deeper, *non?*"

He nodded up at her soberly. She smiled down at him and said, "I doubt you will be lonely, you naughty boy. But confess. Did you feel the *magique,* too?"

He nodded again. She sighed and left. He got up, locked the door, and flopped down again, grinning. He'd been wondering how on earth he was going to bust up with the old gal without feeling guilty. But she'd solved the problem a mite early, in her worldly wisdom. Hell, he still had a hard-on, and he didn't have another soul lined up!

Nothing bad happened in Salt Lake City, so it was sort of tedious for Longarm, even though the City of the Saints treated Sarah Bernhardt well. She switched back to *Camille* in Salt Lake. Playing *Phèdre* wore her out, she said, so she was saving it for Frisco. The only awful thing that took place in Salt Lake was old Lulu's cooking. Longarm didn't mind chop suey for breakfast, but she served it for noon dinner, too.

Lulu said it wasn't chop suey; it was some mighty fancy Indochinese grub. But it tasted like chop suey to Longarm, so at suppertime he decided to be democratic.

Madame Sarah and her intimates ate in the private observation car, but the rest of the troupe ate up forward in the Pullman diner, presided over by a colored gent who'd been taught to cook American. Longarm wanted to get to know the underlings better, in any case, so that evening before the show he went forward to join the cast, musicians, and such.

As he found a vacant place and sat down across from Claudette Laval, a prissy Frenchman Longarm remembered seeing on stage with her and Madame Sarah muttered something in French that sounded surly. Claudette shushed him. But when Longarm tried talking to the gent and discovered he didn't savvy normal conversation, he asked the gal across the table what was eating him.

The pretty brunette shrugged and said, "It is nothing, Monsieur. Paul did not know who you were, and this table is reserved for artists."

"Do tell, ma'am? Well, I'm set now, and I don't see how I'd be any more welcome with the fiddle players or the stagehands, either. So tell him I'm sorry—and could you read this fool menu for me? I can't make heads or tails of it."

"Monsieur does not read French?"

"If I could read it, I could speak it, and tell old Paul, here, what a sissy dude I think he is. Is there anything on that menu that's anything like steak and potatoes, ma'am?"

She laughed, turned to catch the waiter's eye, and ordered for him. The hell of it was that the colored waiter understood her. It sounded mighty awesome, but when they brought his blue plate, it was steak and potatoes, sure enough. He noticed the gal had finished her own food and was lingering over coffee, so he took small bites and made small talk to keep her company. She asked if it was true they were going out across a vast and dangerous desert next. He said, "Well, the Great Basin's vast, ma'am. I can't say it's dangerous near the tracks. The Bannocks are on the reservation and the Paiutes hardly ever throw rocks at the trains no more."

"What about desperadoes, Monsieur Long?"

"A man would have to be desperate, all right, to camp out in the Great Basin at this time of the year. We'll be

140

leaving tonight around one A.M. so by the time you can see anything out your window, there won't be all that much to see. Sunrise ought to catch us just past Elko, going lickety-split along the banks of the Humbolt River, which is only a river when it rains some in the Ruby Mountains. We'll be in Virginia City about noon."

"Ah, we have heard your Virginia City is *très* dangerous, *non?*"

"Shucks, you got good reviews in Cheyenne, didn't you? All big towns are dangerous, ma'am. I've already wired the U. S. Marshal in Virginia City to keep an eye out for suspicious characters."

He didn't add that half the old boys in the tough mining town might well fit that description. She had enough on her mind. The prissy actor next to him must have found it tedious to try to follow the conversation in English. He said something snotty and got up to flounce out.

They both smiled. Longarm asked, "Is old Paul sweet on you, Miss Claudette?" and that made her laugh right out.

She said, *"Mais non.* He is—how you say?—sweet on our trombone player."

"I might have knowed. He sounded sort of snippy just the same. What did he say about me this time?"

"He was not speaking of you; he was teasing me. He seems to think we have been flirting."

"Oh? Have we been flirting, ma'am?"

She smiled down at her coffee and spoke to it in French. Then she looked out the window at the dusty little switch engine passing. "I must return to my compartment. We shall be leaving for the theater any moment."

"You want me to escort you, ma'am?"

"If you wish."

When they got to her door in the next car, she just thanked him and closed the fool door in his face. So he went on back to the observation car to see if the Divine Sarah had been poisoned by the private supper cooked by Lulu.

She must not have. Jarret, Sarah Bernhardt, and Madame Guerard had left for the theater, as far as he could figure

141

out from redheaded Yvette. The Oriental gal spoke more English, but she was sitting down, crying, as the redhead cleaned up. Longarm sat beside her and asked her what was wrong.

She sobbed, "Oh, woe is me! Nobody likes my cooking! Everywhere I am going, I am getting fired. You round-eyed people have such strange tastes, and nobody sells fish sauce over here. How am I to cook without fish sauce?"

He smiled and said, "Come with me, honey. Let's see what they have in the kitchen cupboards."

He led Lulu to the kitchen and sat her down as he explored, relieved to see that most of the cans had been bought over here and so were printed in American. "There's nothing we can do about the coffee," he said. "Madame likes that chicory blend and, as I now see, they ordered the vile stuff from a packer in New Orleans. Let's see—here's mustard, black pepper, salt, and—hot damn, *chili pepper!* We're in luck, Lulu. Now, if I can just find me some red beans, I'll show you how to cook American!"

He did, and there was chopped beef in the icebox. So, as Yvette came to the door to peer in and sniff in wonder, Longarm showed the two maids how to make chili con carne. "The trick is to make it no hotter than it takes to water one's eyes a mite, see?"

Yvette said, *"Merde alors!"* as the smell of hot chili began to rise from the pot on the little stove.

Lulu sniffed. "That smells most formidable, Monsieur."

"You have to let it simmer so's the ingredients marry up some, honey," he told her. "I got to go to the theater now. Just keep that simmering and add enough water from time to time to keep it from charring. Charred chili is awesomely bad. But, by the time everyone comes back from the show tonight, a bowl of hot chili ought to hit the spot. 'Specially after what they had for supper."

He left the gals in charge of the pot and headed over to the theater, where nothing of note happened at all. He'd already seen Camille die. The audience loved it, and none of them acted suspiciously. He met Jarret after the show to tell the Englishman he'd scouted the alley and the coast was clear.

Jarret looked pleased as hell. He waved a newspaper at Longarm and asked, "Have you read the evening papers? That speech Sarah gave in Green River seems to have gone over well indeed. The Ogden critics were kind to us, too. They say Sarah's portrayal of Phèdre was masterful. Do you suppose any of them understood a word she was saying?"

"Don't look gift horses in the mouth, Ed. I told you folks out our way are more cultured than them sissies back East allow. But let's get everybody back to the train, while our luck's holding."

"Agreed. Do you see light at the end of the tunnel, at last?"

"Don't know. Ain't seen anybody trying to blow Madame Sarah up, or shoot her, lately. But the two who tried in Cheyenne were hired killers, not fanatics acting on their own. And last night I met another gun for hire in Ogden. So round up the gals and let's herd 'em home safe."

In less than an hour, Sarah Bernhardt entered her salon, sniffed, and asked, "What on earth is burning in the kitchen? *Sacre bleu!* We really must start searching for another cook."

Longarm said, "Don't fire Lulu yet, ma'am. I put her up to what you smell. Sit down and I'll see if it's ready."

It was, to Longarm's taste, but as the wary Lulu brought the chili con carne out to them all, Madame Sarah grimaced. "Somebody call the fire department! It smells like smoldering gunpowder!"

But she was a good sport in the end and let Lulu serve her a bowl of chili. So Jarret and Madame Guerard had to be good sports, too. Longarm filled his own bowl and sat down expectantly as the Divine Sarah dug in. She tasted, blinked in surprise, and gasped. "Well, it certainly must be good for one's sinuses!" she said. *"Mon Dieu!* None of Doctor Pasteur's fatiguing little germs could live in such an atmosphere!"

"It's rather like curry," Jarret said. "Bit stronger, though."

Madame Sarah swallowed and gulped some coffee. "I think I like it. *Regardez*, I have become an American pioneer woman!" She winked at little Lulu and added, *"Eh bien*, you shall not be shot at sunrise after all. But you must learn more American dishes. I cannot see living on chop suey and chili con carne for the rest of the tour, ma petite."

Longarm said he'd show Lulu how to make flapjacks next. It was getting late. He told Jarret he'd wander the corridors until they were out on the salt flats near Wendover. There was no sense in anyone's standing guard after that. There just wasn't any handy place to rob a train once they watered at Wendover and lit off across the Nevada desert moving downhill and sudden.

He picked up his Winchester by the forward door and moved up the corridor to make sure nobody boarded at the last minute. In a little while he felt the deck thump under his boots and the train started moving. They were winding out around the Great Salt Lake when Jarret passed him, saying that the ladies and their maids had turned in and he aimed to do the same. Longarm headed aft to take up a post on the observation platform, which was still a danger point until the train picked up some speed.

The lamps were out in Madame Sarah's car. He heard the rustle of silk on the other side of Madame Guerard's door. He smiled wistfully, but kept going. He knew womankind well enough to suspicion he could likely talk her into some more loving, if he really tried. But, as it had to end sooner or later in any case, she was doubtless right that they'd skimmed the cream and shouldn't press their luck by getting deeper.

He sat down in one of the wicker chairs out back and lit a cheroot. The moon was full and the train was moving too fast for a mounted man to overtake now. He put the rifle in a corner and put his feet up on the rail to lean back and enjoy a quiet smoke.

It was late, so most of the Mormon homesteads they were passing west of Salt Lake City were dark and quiet, with all those contented families sleeping peaceful. He spied

144

one light in a distant window and wondered idly who was up and why. He hoped it wasn't a sick kid or strange noises in the henhouse. Farm folk had worries, too.

That was what Longarm told himself, every time he was tempted to settle down. Sometimes, passing through a strange town at night, a knockabout gent could get to feeling sorry for himself as he studied on soft lamplight through the curtains of cozy-looking homes. You had to keep remembering that the best of women might snore or turn out to nag once they had a gent roped and branded.

The door slid open behind him. He didn't speak or turn to look. He figured Madame Guerard might have remembered that they hadn't gotten to all the positions yet. He wasn't sure how to handle the situation, so he left it up to her.

But it wasn't Madame Guerard. It was Yvette and Lulu. They were holding hands in their nightgowns and, as the redhead chattered in French, the Oriental gal shyly translated. "Yvette has explained that we should thank you for showing me how to make hot stuff, Monsieur."

"Oh? What does Yvette want to thank me for?"

"She says you make hot stuff in more than one way."

The redhead hiked the skirts of her nightie and forked a leg over Longarm's own stretched-out limbs, to stand facing him with his knees between her thighs as she bent to start unbuttoning his fly. He blinked and said, "For God's sake, ladies! We're passing through settled country in bright moonlight! Tell her to cut that out, Lulu!"

The Oriental gal translated, but Yvette paid her no mind as she hauled out Longarm's organ and commenced to jerk it off. It did seem unlikely that anyone up and about at this hour would see too clearly what might or might not be happening on the blacked-out platform of a passing train.

Longarm said, "Make sure there's nobody in the salon, Lulu!"

"Do not worry, both the older women have retired for the night," Lulu replied.

Then, before Longarm could go into it any deeper with

145

Lulu, he was deep indeed in Yvette. The sassy redhead had lowered herself onto him and was bouncing in time with the clickety-clack of the wheels.

She said something in French. Lulu sighed. "Oh, I saw! I know I too must thank you properly, monsieur, but I am not sure I can take anything that big in poor me!"

"Don't worry about it. Yvette's doing just fine!"

Longarm lay back, closed his eyes, and just enjoyed it, as the roguish redhead showed off for the other gal. Lulu sat in the other chair to watch, and Longarm would have felt even sillier if the light had been better. He knew Lulu couldn't really see anything much, with Yvette's nightgown draped over his lap while her bare bottom bounced up and down with his tool inside her. He wanted to get his own duds out of the way, but it didn't seem decent to take his pants off in public like this. Anyway, it was sort of interesting doing it fully dressed. He hadn't in some time.

Thanks to his earlier activities with Madame Guerard, naked and old-fashioned, Longarm was beaten to the finish line by the randy Yvette. She collapsed on him, throbbing and moaning. He wanted to come himself, but he couldn't, with only the vibration of the wheels to move anything in there.

Yvette suddenly laughed, said something in French, and got off, to leave him sitting there with a raging wet hard-on pointed up at the moon.

Lulu said, "Oh, I *can't!*" But she got up anyway, and moved over as Yvette made room for her. Longarm grabbed her by the hips and Yvette hoisted her skirts to expose her round, tawny bottom in the moonlight. She was too shy to fork a leg over, and Longarm was too comfortable to figure out a better way to work it. So in the end she wound up, with Yvette's help, seated crosswise on Longarm's lap, protesting that he was killing her as she started moving up and down with his rod in her.

He ran his hands up under her thin nightgown to explore her firm body, so different from Yvette's, just now. She giggled as he rolled a nipple between thumb and forefinger.

146

She said, "You men are all alike. Monsieur in San Francisco liked to do it sideways, too. Why do you white men like to do it that way?"

"I figured that might have been the way you got fired by them French folk. Did Madame catch you with the master?"

"*Oui*, but it was not my fault. I am not a wicked girl. I am just weak-natured, *hein?*"

She showed him that there was nothing weak about the rest of her as she leaned forward, arching her back, and began to corkscrew up and down until they were both hissing like steam engines. She moaned that she was coming. He fired up into her hard. Then the door slid open and Madame Sarah said, "Ah, here you all are! What are you children doing out here? Enjoying the night air?"

Yvette murmured something in French, then ducked around Sarah Bernhardt to go to the kitchen for something. Lulu sat frozen in Longarm's lap, with his dick inside her and her gown mercifully covering everything up. Longarm said, "I was talking to Lulu here about flapjacks, ma'am."

Sarah Bernhardt sat down in the other chair. "Go right on, then. I thought you were telling her a bedtime story from the way she is seated."

"Well, I was comforting her, ma'am. She's feeling sort of lost in a strange land."

"I understand. I, too, feel lost out here in this vast expanse of your West. Where are we at the moment, Custis *mon cher?*"

"Coasting along the south shore of the Great Salt Lake, ma'am. Like I was just telling Lulu, here, you can see it if you stare hard, over to the north."

The Divine Sarah leaned forward and stared intently, saying, "Oh, I do think I see moonlight on the water over that way."

Lulu started to rise. Longarm held her down. For, while she wore a gown and Madame Sarah wore a kimono, his fool pecker was outside his fly, and hard!

The Divine Sarah leaned back. "It is hard to see anything

out here, despite the moon," she said. "I am not annoying you, am I, Custis? I could not sleep, but if you two would rather be alone..."

Lulu's tight vagina was pulsating on his erection as she sat there, trying to look innocent. He tried not to move in her at all as he said, "Shucks, we was just discussing flapjacks, ma'am."

"Go right ahead, then. I would like to hear, too."

He said, "Well, like I was saying, Lulu, after you got the batter mixed and the skillet greased, you just make sure they don't burn by flipping 'em over every few minutes."

Lulu said, *"Oui, I flip!"* and sort of bounced on his lap as she made the motion of flipping flapjacks with her hand— damn her devious soul!

Lulu was giggling as she moved just enough to drive him crazy without moving enough for the gal in the other chair to see in the gloom. Longarm knew that if he didn't keep talking, Sarah Bernhardt would wonder why they were still sitting there, so he commenced to lecture them both on how to mix the batter as the platform swayed and vibrated under him, Lulu's innards pulsed and sucked—and, Jesus H. Christ, he was *cominnnnnng!*

"Is something wrong, Custis *mon cher?*" asked Sarah Bernhardt as he ground his teeth and held his breath with Lulu milking his last drops up inside her. He coughed and said, "I must have swallowed some fly ash, ma'am. Startled me some for a second. Thought it was a moth or worse."

"Oh, *mon pauvre!* Lulu, go in and get some water for monsieur like a good girl, *hein?*"

The Oriental gal began to rise, her wet linen clinging to Longarm's erection as she did so.

"Look younder, Miss Sarah!" Longarm said. As the actress turned to follow his gaze, he managed to whip off his hat and drop it in his lap, just in time.

Sarah Bernhardt turned back to him with a puzzled smile. "I saw nothing, Custis."

He was glad to hear that. "I feared you'd miss it," he said. "It was a shooting star, out over the lake."

"Ah, then *you* must make a wish on it, since I did not see it, *hein?*"

He was wishing she'd go inside. Lulu had, so here he sat with the national treasure of France, her in a thin kimono and him with his pecker out of his pants.

But there must have been something in the magic of shooting stars, for after a time she murmured, "Where can that silly maid be with your water?" She got up to duck in and find out. By the time she and Lulu came back out, he had his pants buttoned right. He drank the water with enthusiasm. He hadn't felt so dry-mouthed in quite a spell.

Chapter 12

Longarm had given Lulu all the flapjack lessons she wanted in his own compartment after Madame Sarah went to bed. The next morning he went up to the dining car to have breakfast with the peons. He wanted to get a mite closer to the others in the troupe and he couldn't be eating with the star all the time.

Young Claudette Laval was the only one who spoke enough English to matter, and that gave him a good excuse to corner her some more. The train was rolling fast across a flat sea of gray sage, south of the hazy cottonwood and crack-willow walling in the shallow, sluggish Humbolt River. From time to time they passed a nameless ridge of slanted rimrock, but the Humbolt had been a serious river back when the world was wetter, and none of the rises were close enough to the tracks to worry about.

Claudette had started ahead of him again, which was why he was able to find her sitting alone by the window, sipping coffee. She said she'd just seen either a small antelope or a mighty big jackrabbit. Longarm said that was nice, and added, "I've been meaning to ask you some questions, if you don't mind, Miss Claudette."

He didn't find out anything all that interesting. He already knew that Paul Breguet liked boys, but Claudette said the other two male actors, Catroux and Blanchard, were regular gents, old pros who'd worked with Madame Sarah before. He had to word it delicately, but he was able to get her to tell him finally that the two he-men in the cast were on mighty friendly terms with the other two she-women, Mademoiselles Verde and Granville.

Since he'd had a long, thoughtful look at the remaining actresses, Longarm figured they had to be damned fine lays or else the two Frogs weren't particular. Save for Madame Sarah, herself, Claudette was the only good-looking gal in the bunch up close in daylight.

He sipped at his coffee and said, "It's too bad old Paul is in love with a trombone. Don't you feel sort of left out?"

Claudette made a wry face and replied, "One survives. After my last experience with an actor, I don't care if I ever get involved with another."

"Oh? I thought you might be sort of riled at Madame Sarah for firing that young gent of yours back in Omaha."

She shook her head, lowered her voice, and said, "On the contrary, I was *très* gratified! Don't tell anyone, but it was to save me that Madame sent him packing. Madame is like a mother to me—big sister, at any rate. I am not sure she would like to be thought of as my mother."

"I noticed that she had a thoughtful streak, Miss Claudette. I might have known she'd run him off the spread for getting fresh with a pretty soubrette."

Claudette lowered her eyes. "It was not quite that simple. We began the tour as good friends. Jacques was most handsome and it was easy to become involved with him. Unfortunately, I did not learn until too late that he had a sadistic side."

"You mean he beat you, ma'am?"

"*Oui,* and worse. Madame walked in on us as Jacques was knocking me all over the dressing room. She knocked him all over the dressing room. When he regained consciousness, she had Monsieur Jarret hit him some more and discharge him from the troupe."

Longarm whistled softly. "I figured old Ed Jarret could whip most men, but I'm sort of surprised to learn Madame Sarah's that tough, too!"

Claudette smiled and said, "So was Jacques! He might have escaped with the slap in the face Madame first administered when she came in and found him mistreating me. But he made the mistake of hitting her back with his fist. Madame landed in the corner on her derrière. Then she got up. Have you ever seen a tigress defending her cubs?"

"No. But I get the picture—and I sure wish I'd been there to see it. Did she really knock him out, Miss Claudette?"

"*Oui*. Madame is *très petite*, but, beside being an expert swordswoman, Madame has taken lessons in la savate. It is like your boxing, except that one is allowed to kick."

Longarm chuckled. "I reckon one would have to have been there. Did Sardou have enough to get home on, or did they leave him stranded in Omaha?"

She said, "His passage home was guaranteed, of course. We all signed contracts with Monsieur Jarret before we came to America."

"With Jarret, not Madame Sarah herself?"

"But of course. Monsieur Jarret is the—how you say?—senior partner of this tour. Like us, Madame is more or less working for him. Didn't you know?"

"I do now. Would it be telling family secrets if I got you to give me an educated guess on just what Madame Sarah's getting out of being the national treasure of France, this trip?"

Claudette shrugged. "It is no secret. I saw her contract when I signed my own. Madame is allowed two hundred of your dollars a week for expenses, as well as the private car, servants, and so forth Monsieur Jarret promised. She is guaranteed a thousand additional dollars for each performance, with a bonus if the night's ticket sales run over four thousand, net. Why do you ask? Are you considering an acting career, Monsieur Long?"

"Call me Custis," he said absently, as he mentally added

153

up the numbers of paid for seats he'd counted. "It's no wonder Jarret's so pleased with the good reviews. They must have taken in six or seven thousand last night in Salt Lake."

"*Oui,* it was a full house, and they were very kind. But don't forget, Monsieur Jarret had to pay for the use of the theater, the salaries of the rest of us, and so on. This Pullman special alone is a formidable expense. Frankly, I suspect he is still—how you say—in the red. It is true that we have been playing to packed houses out here, but the first half of the tour, back East, was a total disaster. We must continue to pack them in as we did last night for the rest of the tour, if Monsieur Jarret is to break even, *hein?*"

"Maybe. Do you know if he has an insurance policy covering this tour?"

She shook her head and said she had no idea. His questioning was getting on her nerves, or maybe she had to take a leak, for she suddenly finished her cup, put it down, and said she'd see him in Virginia City. He offered to escort her back to her compartment, but she said not to bother, so he didn't. As he sat back down to finish his eggs, he noticed that she didn't head back to the sleeping cars. She moved forward, toward Jarret's office car up ahead. He shrugged and muttered, "Well, at least the gal is loyal to her employer. Damn it."

They rolled into Virginia City just after high noon. The sun was ready to fry any eggs anyone was dumb enough to bust on the dusty walks. Most of the troupe had sense enough to say in the train. Jarret left to arrange things at the opera house and Longarm headed over to the Western Union. He'd left his frock coat and his fool tie in his quarters. It was hotter than a whore's pillow on Saturday night and nobody from the Denver office could see him in his shirtsleeves and vest at this distance.

A night letter from Billy Vail was waiting for him. Old Billy said that they'd tied at least a few loose strings up for him. The gambling man he'd shot in Denver had been iden-

tified as just what he looked like—a shiftless, drifting tinhorn who'd likely killed that gent in Leadville, like Longarm
had suspicioned. The tinhorn he'd shot in the Greek's at
Odgen matched the description of the Denver gambler's
sidekick. Longarm nodded, partially satisfied. If the two of
them had gunned a man in Leadville, then one of them got
shot by a federal agent in Denver, the survivor figured to
have lit out scared. Meeting the same federal agent in Ogden, unexpected, he'd jumped to the conclusion that he'd
been trailed there, and had gone for his gun.

It just went to show the disadvantages of living with a
guilty conscience. If the fool had simply ordered his ham
and eggs, he'd be alive today.

Having tied that dangler up, old Billy Vail proceeded to
dangle some others with the last part of his night letter. He
said the word on Larimer Street was that the other two,
Smith and Brennen, had been indiscreet enough to confide
in a sporting gal who reported regularly to the Denver police
as a profitable sideline. As Longarm had suspicioned, they'd
been hired to do a heavy job on somebody in Cheyenne.
The whore didn't know who they'd been sent to kill, but
Longarm did, so that part didn't bother him. What bothered
him was that she couldn't say who'd *hired* the sons of
bitches!

He threw the wire in the wastebasket and stepped out
into the glare. The air in Virginia City was so dry and thin
that you didn't feel the heat too much in the shade. But
going outside was like stepping into a furnace.

It couldn't be helped, and the sun would dip below the
rim of the high Sierras to the west later in the day. He
headed for the Virginia City federal building to pay a courtesy call on the local marshal. But, not wanting to show up
all hot and sweaty, he decided to wet his whistle and cool
off a mite first.

It was dark as well as cooler in the saloon near the federal
square. So he didn't see right off who was drinking alone
down the bar as he bellied up and called for anything wet.

The Dorado Kid moved toward Longarm, walking quiet

155

as a cat despite his high-heeled Justins. As Longarm recognized him, the Kid asked, sort of shyly, "Are you following me, Longarm?"

Longarm said, "I was fixing to ask you the same question, Dorado. I thought I left you in Utah. What brings you to Virginia City?"

"I go where I like. It's a free country, ain't it?"

Longarm sighed. "Let's not worry about the Constitution, old son. I can see you didn't take my gentle hint serious. Mayhaps I'd best spell it out for you, Dorado. You're making me proddy as hell. I got enough on my plate without the likes of you offering to be my shadow."

The barkeep slid a schooner of needled beer across the mahogany to Longarm, but Longarm didn't pick it up until he knew just what he meant to fill his hand with.

The Dorado Kid put his own hands on the bar, with his guns out of reach. "Don't try to rawhide me, Longarm," he said. "We both know you won't draw on me unless I gives you just cause. You can't run me out of town. I ain't *done* nothing yet."

"It's the *yet* I'd like to talk to you about, Dorado. You ever hear of a couple of gents named Smith and Brennen? They used to be in your line of work."

The Dorado Kid nodded soberly and said, "I read about you tangling with 'em. It was in the papers. What makes you so mean, Longarm?"

"Gents like you, generally. I don't suppose you heard there's word on the streets that certain parties are in the market for some hired guns?"

"Somebody's always hiring a gun, Longarm. Drink your damned beer. I ain't been hired to go after *you,* damn it!"

That sounded fair, so Longarm picked up the schooner and swallowed some cool suds. He put it down with a sigh and said, "Jesus, it's hot today, ain't it? Would you like to tell me who you are gunning for, Dorado?"

The Dorado Kid just smiled sardonically. Longarm said, "I know your rep, Dorado. You likely wouldn't gun a woman unless somebody really made it worth your while. You don't

156

even gun men cheap. Let's see now. When's the last time you were in Denver?"

"Did I say I'd been in Denver, Longarm?"

"Nope, but I'd be surprised if you told a lawman the truth when the truth was in your favor. I can find out if you've been loitering on Larimer Street of late, you know."

The Dorado Kid shrugged. "Go ahead, then. It's been nice meeting up with you again, Longarm. But *you* make *me* nervous, too!"

Longarm finished his drink morosely as the Dorado Kid strode out, bold as brass. Longarm knew the son of a bitch had him figured right as a gent who couldn't kill in cold blood without a sensible reason to give the coroner's jury. It gave the hired gun a hell of an edge on him.

But the conversation hadn't been entirely wasted. He'd caught the uneasy flicker in the killer's oyster-gray eyes when he'd mentioned Denver. Smith and Brennen had been hired by someone in Denver. The only trouble was, Madame Sarah Bernhardt and her troupe had never been anywhere near Denver yet, and weren't planning to appear there on this trip.

He finished his beer, told the empty schooner it didn't make sense, and went on over to the Virginia City marshal's office. They were friendlier than the clerk in Ogden, and allowed they could spare a few deputies that evening if Longarm could rustle up a few free passes to the show. He asked if they'd heard anything from their own informants about a call-up of hired guns. They said they hadn't, the ignorant sons of bitches.

Longarm had better luck at Madam Lavinia's Boarding House for Single Working Girls. A colored maid ushered him into the madam's ruby room and old Lavinia invited him to take off his duds and stay a spell.

Longarm sat down on the bed with her and said it was too hot. Madam Lavinia said that was why she was walking about in nothing but her long black stockings and red garters. She got up to build them a couple of cool drinks as he admired her rear view. Madam Lavinia had come west to

157

mine the Comstock Lode by letting gents probe her own depths some. He knew the blonde hair was a wig and that she shaved her pubic hair to keep the gray from showing. But she looked all right from behind as she mixed gin and lemonade while he told her what he was looking for.

She turned and came back to the bed with the drinks. She sat down beside him again and handed him his glass, saying, "It's funny you should mention a party in Denver looking to hire hardcases, Custis. One of my girls was telling me about that just this morning. You know I runs a respectable joint, and I don't hold with law-breaking."

"I know, Lavinia. You always were one for law and order. That's why I came to you. What did your—ah—employee say?"

"A customer last night said he'd just come in from Denver. He'd been drinking downstairs a spell, trying to make up his mind or get up his pecker—whatever. He must have been really drunk by the time they got up to her crib. He wanted to spend the night. When she told him how much extra it would cost him, he asked for credit. Told her he was fixing to get paid a lot of money, see?"

"Paid by someone in Denver for gunning somebody here?"

"You got it. We don't give credit, of course, but knowing I sometimes sell favors to the law, my gal let him stay a little extra, whilst she pumped him both ways. She didn't get the whole story. He wasn't *that* drunk. But it seems some rich gent in Denver hired him to come over here and gun somebody important. Naturally, he said he couldn't tell her who. Just that he was getting a thousand dollars for the job, and that if she was nice to him, he'd make it up to her."

"Could your gal tell if the man in Denver was a foreigner? The party I'm concerned about could have political enemies in France."

"Oh, are you with Sarah Bernhardt, Longarm? I was wondering what brung you to Virginia City, since you don't want to lay *me*."

"Never mind who I might or might not want to play slap

158

and tickle with, Lavinia. I asked about the mystery man in Denver."

"The owlhoot never said he was a Frenchman. Just said he was a Denver big shot. What are they after your gal for in France?"

He sipped his drink, frowned, and said, "They likely ain't. If anyone in France was out to murder her, they'd have done so there, long before now. But, damn it, nobody on *this* side of the pond has a sensible reason for harming her neither."

Madam Lavinia sipped her own drink. "Look for a reason that *ain't* sensible, then," she said. "Half the troubles in this world are caused by boobs and idjets, honey. Are you sure you don't feel horny? *I* sure do."

He patted her plump thigh, to be polite, as he said, "I wish I had the time, Lavinia. Listen, this gent who talks so much in shell-like ears wasn't a tall, dark jasper all dressed in black, was he?"

She shook her blonde wig. "Nope. He was short and dressed in denim. Looked like a stunted cowhand."

Longarm drained the glass, set it down, and got to his feet, saying, "That makes *two* I'll likely know on sight. It was a two-man team in Ogden, too. You've been a great help, Lavinia. I thank you, but I got to get it on down the road."

He placed a gold coin on her dresser, by the door, as the naked old whore lay back, spread her thighs, and asked, "'Fess up. Don't this tempt you at all, honey?"

He laughed and said it surely did. Then he left before he could get in trouble. It wasn't that he was too proud to lay a pro, free, but a man had to draw the line *some* infernal where!

Leaving the whorehouse, Longarm paid another courtesy call on the Virginia City law. They said they could provide some help in and about the opera house that night, but they hadn't heard a thing about two known hired guns being in town. It just went to prove that crooks talked more to naked womenfolk than to copper badges.

He went to the opera house. He told the old stage-door man who he was and was allowed inside. The stage-door man called a young Paiute with a broom over and told the boy to show Longarm around, adding that he'd just missed Edward Jarret. The Divine Sarah's manager and some gents from the front office had left to have a drink on their deal for later that night.

Longarm followed the Indian kid about the premises. There wasn't much to see. The scenery hadn't been sent over from the train yet, so the backstage area was bare of all but sandbags, ropes, and such. The dressing rooms were spartan, but nobody had planted any bombs in any of them. He asked the Paiute if there was any handy way to slip in and out of the barn-like opera house, sneaky. The Indian shook his head and said the walls were solid brick and all the doors were oak, sheathed with sheet iron to be fireproof and burglarproof as well.

Longarm went out front, got down on his hands and knees, and crawled up the aisle, peering under the fold-up seats. The Paiute asked what in the hell he expected to find there. Longarm said, "Sometimes a gent's been known to tape a weapon or worse to the bottom of a seat ahead of time. That way, patting folk down at the entrance of an evening don't work, see?"

"You're wasting your time. Nobody's been in here. Nobody's going to get past Pop, at the stage door, neither."

Longarm checked out the seats anyway, got to his feet, and asked if he could go out the front way. The Indian said he couldn't. The front doors and the fire exits were all padlocked on the inside and would stay that way until evening. Longarm nodded, satisfied, and left via the stage door.

The alley out to the street was long and narrow, but a guard posted at each end could take care of that worry. One wall of the alley was the rear of the opera house itself. The other wall was lower, being the back walls of stores facing the street at the end of the block. The stores would all be shut that night.

He was almost out of the alley when he ran into Claudette

Laval going the other way. He stopped her and said, "You missed Ed Jarret, if that's who you're looking for, Miss Claudette."

"As a matter of fact, I've been looking for a place to take a bath," she said. "The shower at the end of my car is not working. I think the tank must be empty, *non?*"

"It likely is. You have to get under a train shower ahead of everyone else on a day like this. As hot as it is, I'm surprised I got one myself this morning. There ain't no bath or shower in the opera house, ma'am. I just got done exploring the layout."

"C'est atroce! What am I to do? I must have a bath before I change into my costume this evening. It is still but early afternoon and I am already perspiring like a little piggie!"

He thought for a moment, then said, "I know a place just down the street where you could likely get washed up, ma'am. It's a new hotel that's up to date with all the latest improvements."

He took her by the elbow and led her out of the alley. She frowned and asked, "Are you suggesting we check into a *hotel*, Custis?"

"Not hardly. We got bunks to spare aboard the special. The manager's a pal of mine. I'll just tell him you want to use one of his empty rooms to take a bath, and he won't charge you, long as you're with me."

She was giggling as he took her into the hotel and up to the desk. He asked for the manager he knew, but the snooty room clerk said he'd left for the day. Longarm snorted in annoyance. "All right. How much does a room with a bath hire for by the hour?" he asked.

The clerk looked startled, stared at Claudette, and lowered his eyes to stammer, "We don't rent rooms by the *hour*, sir. I can let you have a double for a dollar if you'd care to register."

Claudette was tugging at his shirtsleeve and trying to tell him something. But Longarm put a cartwheel down on the marble counter. "Gimme the key, then. We ain't fixing to

161

register, 'cause we won't be staying that long. Just tell old Tom, when he gets back, that Deputy Custis Long was here."

The clerk wasn't man enough to argue with Longarm. He handed him the key to a room on the second floor. Longarm turned to Claudette and said, "There you go. I'd best go up with you and unlock the door."

As he escorted her up the stairs she gave a stifled laugh and asked, "Don't you realize what that must have looked like to that poor boy?"

"I don't care," he said. "If he had a lick of sense he wouldn't have charged us the use of the infernal bath in the first place."

"But, Custis, he must think we are lovers!"

"Well, that's nothing to be ashamed of, neither. Neither one of us is bad-looking and we're both white folks of opposing genders. Things could have been worse. We could have been old Paul and his trombone player, right?"

She laughed. "You are a very naughty boy! Are you sure you have not lured me up here to have your wicked way with me, Custis?"

He unlocked the door, ushered her in, and surveyed the small clean room and big brass bedstead. "I hardly ever trick gals, ma'am. Yonder's the bath, through that doorway."

"Hmm, I see that the door has no lock on it, Custis."

"Well, they likely figure anyone checking in here together sees no need to lock themselves in the bathroom. This ain't the honeymoon suite. You go ahead and lather up, Miss Claudette. I'll sit out here and smoke whilst you bathe. Then, if you ain't in a hurry, I may just have *me* a bath, too. There's nothing like a hot soak in a real tub to get the road grime out of your hide."

She moved over to the doorway, turned coyly, and asked, "Can I trust you, Custis?"

"Trust me about what? Busting in on you while you're in the tub? I ain't that desperate—no offense. I can generally be trusted about as far as the lady I'm with wants to trust me."

"Ah? May one assume that sometimes other women tempt you?"

"Hell, girl, *all* women tempt me. *I* ain't no trombone player. Go on and take your infernal bath. I said I wouldn't peek."

She closed the door, laughing silly as hell, and he sat down on the bed and fished out a smoke as she ran her hot bath. He tried not to picture what was going on in there as he heard the soft slither of silk behind the thin door panels. Had he known he was going to wind up in a fix like this he'd have taken Madam Lavinia up on her kind offer earlier. It was a pain in the ass to get a hard-on so early in the day.

He awaited the sounds of splashing after he heard Claudette turn off the taps. But she was mighty quiet in there for a spell. The door opened and she came back out. Her dark hair was pinned up and she'd wrapped a hotel towel around her. It was a small towel, he could see that she was blushing all over.

He said, "Ma'am?"

"The water is too hot," she said. "The cold tap does not work. I must wait until the tub cools a bit, *non?*"

He said that sounded reasonable and snuffed out his smoke as she sat on the bed beside him. But, when he took her in his arms, she gasped, "Why, Monsieur, whatever do you think you're doing?"

He didn't answer as he kissed her and lowered her back across the bed, getting rid of his hat and gun rig with his free hand as she tongued him back, rubbing her bare knees together.

As he started shucking her out of the towel, Claudette stopped kissing him and protested, "But I have not yet bathed! We are both still dirty!"

"Dirty can be fun. We'll take a bath together after, honey."

"Oh, dear, this is all so—so sudden! Whatever gave you the idea you could be so forward with me, Custis, *mon cher?*"

He was too polite to tell her *she* had. He never would have busted in on her bare-assed. But all bets were off when a gal busted *out* bare-assed to a healthy man. She must have

163

known the rules, too. For, despite all the dumb things she was saying, Claudette went for his top buttons as he went to work on the bottom ones. And for a gal who swore she never would have come here with him had she known his evil designs, she sure acted like he was forgiven once he was in her.

She locked her bare ankles around the nape of his neck and reached for a pillow to shove under her own rump as he commenced to pound her. He knew she'd told him true about not having done this since Omaha. It began to feel like he hadn't, either. She was built nothing like Yvette or Lulu, and the strange surroundings inspired him to new heights. She groaned, *"Sacre bleu, there is so much of you and so little of me!"*

"Am I hurting you, honey?"

"I did not say that. It feels marvelous. I've just never done it with a horse before, and . . . *ooh la la, c'est fantastique!* And I am . . . Ahhhhh!"

He came, too. Then, seeing they were old pards now, he took time out to take off the last of his duds, including his socks. She was spread out on the unfolded towel. It was just as well for the bedspread that she was. She sniffled and said, "Let us take a bath together, as you suggested."

So they did, and as she lay under him in the warm water, Claudette said that now she knew what a seal would feel like doing it with a walrus. She did feel sort of slick and seal-slithery under him as he came in her under the water and they both damned near drowned.

They got out to finish right, clean and wet across the bed, and to hell with the spread. He'd paid a whole damned dollar and most of it would dry anyway.

Claudette wanted to get on top. Then, after they'd done it that way, she felt relaxed enough with him to suggest some other variations. By the time they stopped, around three-thirty or four, each knew the other's body as well as their own. Better, maybe. He wondered what in thunder she and her sadistic ex-boyfriend could have had to fight about after she begged him to tie her upside down to the brass bedboard. But he didn't ask her how she'd learned to screw so wild. After they'd had another bath and were getting dressed, Claudette started sniffling and begging him never to tell on her. He said he wouldn't. He was starting to savvy what these French gals meant by "practical." It seemed that anything went as long as nobody gossipped about it afterwards.

Chapter 13

Nobody seemed to pay them any mind as Longarm took Claudette back to the special. As he'd hoped, by late afternoon the cruel Nevada sun had dropped below the black jagged rim of the high Sierras long before most towns expected sundown. The sky stayed light, which was sort of spooky, as though it were a bright, cloudless day with no sun in the sky. But Virginia City's early sunsets tended to make Virginia City's nights black as the pit, and the moon would be setting, too, by the time the show was over that night.

Nothing happened on the way to the theater, or during another performance of *Camille,* as Americans insisted on calling it.

The audience of mostly hard-rock miners and their families had paid good money to see the Divine Sarah die, and they applauded like hell when she did. But, while dying up on stage was only doing her duty, Longarm didn't consider it fair to expect her to die offstage and for real. So he stepped out into the alley before the final curtain to ask one of the other deputies there if he'd noticed anything.

The lawman shook his head and said, "Not so much as a stray cat. Mike Billings was just here. He says him and the others free to prowl has searched high and low for the

Dorado Kid and the short, stubby sidekick he might have."

"And?"

"And nothing. If they're still in Virginia City, they must be hiding under a rock. They can't be found on or off the streets tonight."

Longarm swore and said, "They ain't inside. I've checked the audience till they must think I'm an usher. Who's down at the far end?"

"Pete Mahoney. Local copper. He's all right. Oh, I almost forgot. They told me to give this to you, Longarm."

He handed Longarm a yellow envelope. Longarm tore open the wire and held the message up to the light from the stage door, to read that Billy Vail had some important things to tell him. Longarm was off the case as soon as a brace of Secret Service agents arrived to relieve him.

It seemed the folk in Washington had had second thoughts after reading about how Sarah Bernhardt had saluted the flag in Green River, and likely how many voters out West were crowding in to applaud and stomp their boots for her.

The other important thing was that Billy had solved the case, or thought he had. Jacques Sardou, a French national, had been arrested in a Larimer Street saloon after one of the gents he thought he was hiring to gun Madame Sarah Bernhardt turned out to be a police informer. Claudette had said her old boyfriend was a sadist, and he was rich besides, so it fit.

There was just one thing wrong with Billy's solution. Sardou might be in jail in Denver, but the killers he'd sent to gun the Divine Sarah here in Virginia City weren't. They wouldn't know the deal was off. They'd been promised a thousand each to do in the national treasure of France as best they could—and the Dorado Kid was one of the best.

He told the other deputy about the contents of the wire and added that they were still stuck with the chore until a posse of Secret Service agents could arrive. Then he went back inside to wait for Madame Sarah and the others.

He didn't have long to wait. It was a long haul from Virginia City to Frisco, and Jarret had arranged an early start with no cast party after the show in Virginia City. When he heard them coming like a gaggle of geese, Longarm consulted his watch, blinked in surprise, and reset it with a sheepish grin as he remembered they were on Pacific Time now, and it wasn't really *that* early.

He blocked the doorway until the whole troupe was backed up in front of him like the waters of a dam. He held up a hand for silence, but he didn't get much. French folk sure liked to talk a lot. Finally he shouted, "Jarret, make sure the gals is in the middle, with gents all about. I got us covered as we leave the opera house, and there's more deputies about the railyards and staked out along the way. But it's still a far piece and it's dark as hell outside. If the balloon goes up and I get busy, I'm depending on you to herd these folk back inside the opera house or run 'em for the train, depending on how far we've convoyed 'em. You got that, Ed?"

Jarret spoke rapid-fire French to his charges, then called back, "Lead on."

Longarm slid open the stage door and stepped out first. The lamp over the door had gone out. He squinted up the long, dark alley and saw someone standing at the entrance with a long-gun at port arms. But he didn't see the deputy who was supposed to be here by the door. He called out, "Is that you, Mahoney?" and the distant figure replied, "Yeah. What's up?"

"We're missing a deputy here. Did you see him leave and did he say why?"

"Nope. Nobody's got past me either way, Longarm."

Longarm frowned and called to Jarret, "Hold it, Ed. We need some light on the subject before we make our next move."

But even as Longarm was striking a light, the damn fool actors were spilling out the doorway like kids getting out of school for the day. As Longarm's match flared, he saw a figure across the alley, face down against the far wall, with a staghorn knife handle rising from between his shoulder blades.

169

Then a voice called out, "Longarm! Above you!" Longarm let go of the match and threw himself sideways to the alley pavement as a bullet whip-cracked through the space he'd just been filling.

After that, it got even more confusing. Longarm landed on his side and rolled as another bullet spanged off the brick paving where he'd have been if he'd just stayed there like a greenhorn. He rolled back over the rising brick dust to let the rifleman on the roof above waste a third shot in anticipation of where he *might* have rolled!

Other guns were going off all around. The gals were screaming between the shots as the echoing alley filled with smoke. It looked like London on a foggy night by the time Longarm was on his feet again with gun in hand. But he could see the sky above, so, as a star winked out, he fired at whoever was atop the roof across the alley and was rewarded with a scream of pain and the sounds of falling metal and meat as the star winked on again.

Then it got mighty quiet. Jarret had herded the others back and was standing by the doorway, his own gun drawn, as he whispered, "See anything, Longarm?"

Longarm said, "Nope. Stay put while the smoke clears." Then he called, "Hey, Dorado?"

A sort of choked-up voice replied, "I'm over here. I'm down. I got one of the bastards. How about you?"

"I got one, too. How many were there, Kid?"

"Two was all I counted. Is Miss Bernhardt all right?"

Longarm could see better now. He moved down the alley to where the Dorado Kid lay near the open rear door of a deserted shop.

"Nobody else on our side was shot, thanks to you, Kid," he said. He yelled for Jarret to relight the alley lamp as he hunkered by the wounded gunslick and observed, "You could have saved me some needless worry had you told me whose side you were on, Dorado. But I thank you for that timely word of warning anyhow. How badly are you hit?"

"Serious. I was never on *your* side, damn it. I heard talk that some son of a bitch had put a price on Miss Sarah's pretty head. I couldn't go to the law with it. That ain't in my code. But how could I let 'em gun such a swell little gal?"

The alley lit up as Jarret lit the lamp by the stage door. Longarm could see other bodies now. Near the deputy they'd knifed in the back lay a stubby gent in faded denim, who'd followed his rifle off the roof. Up near the alley entrance lay a corpse in blue and the lookout who'd slickered Longarm by pretending to be the law, after taking out the real law and putting out the lights. He knew that was the rascal who'd hulled the Dorado Kid, and vice versa.

He opened the Kid's black jacket and grimaced down at the blood pulsing out of the black shirt. "It don't look so good, Dorado," he said. "Is there anybody you want us to get in touch with after?"

"Not hardly, thanks. I run away from home when I was fourteen. I sure hope my family thinks I died in the War. My folk were sort of religious. But I'd surely like to meet up with Miss Sarah Bernhardt before I cashes in my chips, Longarm."

Longarm wasn't sure it was such a good notion. But the Divine Sarah had heard as she stepped out into the alley. She came right over, kilted her skirts up, and knelt down to take the Dorado Kid's hand in hers.

"I am here, monsieur. I am at a loss for words to thank you for your gallantry. Won't you introduce us, Custis?"

"Yes'm. Madame Sarah Bernhardt, this here's the Dorado Kid. Kid, this here's Madame Sarah Bernhardt—in the living flesh, thanks to you."

The Dorado Kid gazed up at her, his eyes already starting to glaze. "I can't see you clear, ma'am. But it sure makes me proud to meet up with you personal like this."

"Custis," she murmured, "we must get a doctor, *non?*"

Longarm didn't reply.

The Dorado Kid said, "Doctor wouldn't be able to help much now, ma'am. But don't worry yourself about me. I never was worth much. I always knowed I'd end like this, Miss Sarah. But if I helped to save you, my life wasn't wasted, so what the hell."

A tear ran down her cheek as she pressed his hand to

171

her breast and asked him, "Why did you do it, Monsieur Kid? I meant nothing to you. We never met before."

The Dorado Kid said, "I knew who and what you was, ma'am. I never seen you act. Now I never will. But I'm proud of you anyway. You showed the snooty bastards by making it big, while making it clean and honest. You took 'em all on, fair and square, and you *won*. That's more'n I can say. But, when push comes to shove, our kind has to stick together. So when I heard they was gunning for you, I done what I could."

Longarm had no idea what the dying man was talking about. But Sarah Bernhardt nodded soberly and said, "If I am to sit shiva for you, I must know your real name. Whoever heard of sitting shiva for such a person as a Dorado Kid, *hein?*"

He smiled crookedly and murmured, "Dorado is Spanish for my real name, which is Goldman, ma'am. But don't trouble yourself with Jewish services for the likes of me. I've never been a decent Jew—or anything else worth mention."

She leaned forward to kiss his dying lips as she murmured, "You are wrong, Monsieur Goldman." Then she straightened up and told Longarm, "I think he is dead. Do you suppose he heard me, Custis?"

"I'm sure he did, ma'am. But now we have to get you all back to the railyards, pronto."

As he helped Sarah Bernhardt to her feet, some other gents came down the alley from the street. Longarm saw light flash on a copper badge and knew they'd responded to the sounds of gunplay. So he asked them to clean up the mess and they said they would. Jarret joined him to ask the next move. Longarm said he reckoned it was over, but to keep his gun handy anyway. As they all headed for the railyards together, he filled Jarret and Sarah Bernhardt in on the message from Denver, assuring them that he'd stay with them until the Secret Service caught up.

The railyards weren't far, and nothing happened along the way. But as they spotted the lights in the windows of the Pullman special and headed across the tracks for them, a bright orange blossom of flame exploded in their faces.

Longarm grabbed Sarah Bernhardt and shielded her with his body as bits and pieces of shattered wood fluttered down on them out of the rising smoke plume blotting out the stars above the special's siding.

He let go of her and started running toward the observation car as soon as he saw that nothing serious enough to hurt was coming down. Behind him, Jarret called out a question. Longarm shot back, "Hold the herd there while I see what happened!"

When he hauled himself over the platform railing and ducked inside, the salon was filled with the acrid fumes of dynamite and both Yvette and Lulu were screaming fit to bust in the dark.

He struck a match and lit a table lamp. He picked it up and made his way forward to join the maids in the companionway between the kitchen and Sarah Bernhardt's door. The kitchen was still there, but the Divine Sarah's compartment had been blasted all to hell.

The windows, part of the side wall, and half of the roof were missing. The scorched deck was covered with feather ticking and smoldering rags. He started stomping them out as he figured out where the bomb had been placed. It had gone off directly under Sarah Bernhardt's bed.

The Dorado Kid had saved her life twice that night. Had not it been for the delay at the opera house, the national treasure of France would have been just about in bed when the infernal device went off.

He called out of the hole in the side of the car and Jarret herded the awed road company over. While they were climbing aboard, Longarm moved to the still-intact, albeit scorched, dressing table against the surviving bulkhead and held the lamp high as he slid open drawers. He found a rosewood jewel case and opened it. The Tear of Dumas winked up at him by lamplight. So they hadn't been out to rob her.

Jarret, Madame Sarah, and Madame Guerard came in. Jarret whistled and Sarah Bernhardt gasped, *"Mon Dieu! I thought you said it was over, Custis!"*

Longarm shrugged and said, "I thought it was. Reckon you'll have to sleep forward till they can repair this mess or, more likely, furnish another car, ma'am. Your jewels weren't hurt by the blast. Diamonds are tougher than folk."

"Never mind about my possessions, Custis *mon cher*. It is my *derrière* that I cannot replace, and if I had been sitting on the bed just now . . ."

"We have to find out who did it, Longarm!" Jarret said. "It couldn't have been anyone who was at the theater with us just now, but . . ."

"I'm ahead of you." Longarm stepped out into the corridor to hail the frightened maids.

He wasn't surprised that neither of them could remember anybody putting dynamite under Madame Sarah's bed in front of them. He doubted either Yvette or Lulu had done it. Neither was all that bright, but neither would have been dumb enough to stay in the same car if they'd known an infernal device was ticking away in the next compartment. Dynamite was tricky stuff. Though the two young gals had only been scared out of a year's growth by the blast, they'd been lucky.

Latour, the butler, had been at the opera house with the others that evening. As he moved up the line to question the American train crew, they all seemed to alibi one another. All said they'd never gone aft to the observation car, since they'd had no call to. By this time, of course, the yard boss and his bulls had gathered about, and none of them recalled any mysterious figures loitering about the special. Some of them were leading dogs, and that made it seem even more unlikely that a stranger had slipped past them.

By the time Longarm had satisfied himself that there were no easy answers, the dispatcher had ordered the busted-up car uncoupled and hauled off to the repair shed—after making sure Madame and her servants had moved out all their possibles, of course.

Jarret said Madame Sarah and her companion, Madame Guerard, could bunk in his compartment while he stood guard outside the door. He said his insurance would cover the wrecked car. But that, since nobody would insure the profits and losses of a theatrical tour, he meant to see Madame Sarah appeared alive and well in Frisco, where the tickets were already sold.

Longarm felt sort of wistful about that. He knew he'd be leaving the company almost any time now, and he'd hoped for a more tender farewell from Madame Guerard. Having sampled most of the possibilities on hand, he knew she was still the best in the bunch.

Yvette and little Lulu were just play-pretties to have fun with. Old Claudette was beautiful and mighty passionate, but she acted more strange than loving in bed, and he felt the need of some soft, sweet love to settle his nerves right now. Madame Guerard looked sort of wistful, too, as they said good night.

As she moved off, silent, up the corridor, Madame Sarah made up for her older sidekick's shyness by saying good night to Longarm right. She threw her arms about him and kissed him smack on the lips. Being human, he kissed back with enthusiasm. She was light as a feather in his arms, but her firm little breasts against his chest told him she was tough enough to handle any man in bed. He was wondering if he should tongue her when she leaned her face away, eyes mocking, and said, *"Eh bien,* I admire the way you are—ah—growing up! But we had better have mercy on ourselves, *non?"*

He let her go and she scampered after Madame Guerard, skipping like a young gal with a secret. Edward Jarret was frowning as he muttered, "I say, she seems unusually fond of you this evening, Longarm."

"That's all right, Ed. I'm fond of her. But don't get your bowels in an uproar. I'll be heading back to Denver as soon as the Secret Service catches up with us. I doubt like hell any of them sissy Secret Service agents will make a play for your girl."

"My girl? Are you implying Sarah Bernhardt's in love with me, you idiot?"

"Nope. But it's plain to see you're in love with her, Ed. It ain't for me to say how you two work it out, though. You're on your own."

Chapter 14

Longarm lay naked in his bunk as the special wound through the high Sierras. He'd left the door unlatched, so he wasn't surprised when it opened in the dark. He'd figured *somebody* was bound to sneak in to join him. The real fun part would come after, but it was sort of fun to wonder who liked him best, too.

He hoped it would be Yvette or Lulu, but he was game for Claudette, if she wanted some more gentle torture.

He could tell that it was two gals. They were giggling and whispering to each other in French. But as they shucked their robes and climbed in naked on either side of him, neither one felt at all like the redhead or the Oriental gal. One was fat and the other was skinny. He tried to ask them who the hell they might be, but the fat one kissed him as the skinny one went down on him. So he gave up and just enjoyed it as it came to him and he came in them.

They were the left-over actresses he'd dismissed as plain after Claudette told him they were both taken. He'd forgotten which was which or who was the ugliest, but it didn't matter in the dark, and even if they had boyfriends, as Claudette had said, they seemed to share his taste for variety. He knew the whole crew had been crowded together some after losing the one car. He couldn't figure out if they'd heard about him from Claudette or the two randy maids, but apparently it paid to advertise. Someone had surely praised his skill to them, for they couldn't seem to get enough of it.

It was nice but sort of spooky, making love to two strangers he couldn't see or speak with. The skinny one seemed to be the ringmaster and, since the fat one understood her suggestions better than Longarm did, the position changes kept coming as delightful surprises. As the trucks click-clacked them through the darkness he wound up with his back to the bulkhead and somehow screwing both of them at once. He couldn't figure out how they'd worked it, for there was thigh and rump no matter where he felt, but they'd gotten sideways to him, belly to belly, with their legs tangled like denning snakes, so that his shaft was gripped between both their moist slits while massaging both their clits as he pumped it sideways in—or at—them. All three came together. Then he felt the real thing of the skinny one engulfing him to milk the last drops. Only, when he held her closer, it turned out that he was in the fat one. It didn't matter. She came ahead of him, this time. so he finished in the skinny one.

They left before it got light enough to see which one was the ugliest. It was just as well. By now he was sure he'd been a mite mistaken about their looks. Nobody that ugly could have screwed so pretty.

He struck a match to see what time it was after they'd left and laughed. It was only a little after three, early enough still to catch some shuteye before the train stopped at Sacramento. On the other hand, he wasn't tired enough to sleep, with all the things he had on his mind to keep him awake. So he lit a smoke and just lay there listening to the wheels as the train highballed through the night.

He'd just finished and snubbed out the cheroot when the door slid open softly again and Claudette's voice whispered, "Are you awake, *mon cher?*"

He said, "Yep. Ain't got a bathtub in here, though."

She giggled and sat down beside him, slipping out of

178

her robe. "I waited to make sure everyone else was tucked in for the night." She sniffed. "What's that I smell? Have you been naughty, Custis? This compartment reeks of cheap tobacco, expensive perfume, and—ah—body odor."

"Well, I plead guilty to the three-for-a-nickel smokes. I got a body too. Now that you mention it, it does smell she-male in here. I reckon some gal must have been in here a spell back. Maybe two gals. No one gal would wear that much stink-pretty, right?"

She slid in beside him, saying, "I know how to find out if you've been naughty." Then, as he rose to the occasion when she fondled his shaft, she laughed. "I see you *have* been waiting for me, *hein?*"

"I was sort of hoping you might see fit to join me, Claudette."

So she joined him, getting on top for openers. He was surprised how good it felt, considering. But as she started moving up and down with her tight flesh milking him, he decided she was mighty pretty, too. It was another change to fondle someone in the dark he'd recognized in broad day, and Claudette was built smack in between the fat and skinny gals who'd just left. So that was different, too. But somehow, while he could still keep it up, he couldn't really get all the way over the hump this time, even when Claudette came and begged for more.

He rolled her over to do it right, posting in the saddle to be polite, but starting to feel jaded. He wanted to come again, if only so he could stop for a spell. But even doing it to the prettiest gal in the troupe could turn into a chore once the bloom was off the rose. So he just said he was coming and, after that made her explode under him, he rolled off.

"You are formidable!" she said as she lay beside him, fondling his semi-erection. After a while, she said, "It is still hard. Can we do it again, *mon cher?*"

"In a minute. I gotta get my second wind."

She giggled and got on top again, saying, "I know what will excite you!"

She was right.

He wanted her to sleep with him, afterward. But after they'd washed up at the sink in the corner and finished by doing it again, standing naked against the swaying bulkhead, Claudette said she had to be in her own compartment when they came to wake her. So, after she left, Longarm locked the door. He just wasn't up to any more surprises, pleasant or otherwise.

There was no show planned for Sacramento, but the train had to stop there anyway to switch the special over to the Southern Pacific switcher that would run them around the bay to Frisco.

That was where the Secret Service caught up with Longarm. They'd ridden the switcher out from Frisco after getting wired instructions from D. C.

There were four of them, dressed San Francisco style, but otherwise looking sensible. They showed Longarm their orders and told him he was free to head back to Denver on the next eastbound. Longarm took them to meet the manager. Jarret said they'd have to wait to meet Madame Sarah, as she was still asleep up forward. They said that was jake with them. They'd be traveling with her all the way now.

Jarret held out a hand to Longarm. "I guess this is good-bye, then, Longarm. I can't tell you how grateful we all are, and if there's anything I can ever do for you..."

"I've got one favor, Ed. Is Mademoiselle Claudette awake yet?"

"I don't think so. Did you want to see her before you left?"

"Not hardly. There's no hurry, and these gents can arrest her when she gets to Frisco. Save a lot of bother that way."

He saw they were all looking at him sort of thunder-gasted, so he said, "Oh, that's right—I hadn't told anybody about *her*, yet. She's the one who planted the bomb under Madame Sarah's bed last night."

Jarret gasped, "Are you mad? She was at the opera house with us last night! She was standing near me when the bomb went off across the yard!"

180

"Sure she was, Ed. You see, she went to the opera house early to plant it in Madame Sarah's dressing room. Only I ran into her, so the excuse she had for going to the theater early wouldn't work. She must have had it in her bag. Anyway, after we got back to the train, she reset it and put it under Madame Sarah's bunk when nobody was looking. She set it to go off after Madame Sarah got back and went to bed. But, not knowing you had to set your clock back as you go west, she had it set just too early!"

"My God! That's monstrous! But can you prove any of your charges, Longarm?"

"Sure. Elimination. She had the motive. Madame Sarah fired her sadistic boyfriend, Sardou, and we already know that *he* took it mighty serious. A gal loco enough to go to bed with a he-brute like Sardou had to be just as mean-natured. She likely missed him. It's hard to get other gents to sadist you right after you've had a sample of the real thing. Nobody else in the company had such a motive. Nobody else tried to sneak into a locked-up opera house. Nobody but one of the actors could have snuck into Madame Sarah's private car, neither. What do you boys want, eggs in your beer? She'll likely confess once she's arrested. I *can't* arrest her. That's how come I know she has a sort of hysterical streak a good prosecutor can likely get a story outten."

A couple of the Secret Service agents looked convinced. But Jarret said, "Wait—have you forgotten she was in the alley last night with the rest of us when those gun thugs opened up on you?"

Longarm said, "She and her boyfriend was working at cross purposes. Sardou stayed in Denver after sending his hired guns after Madame Sarah. He wasn't in communication with his crazy sweetheart. Claudette was working on her own to kill the Divine Sarah. She got the idea of blowing her up when the first attempt by the other two hired killers failed in Cheyenne."

"But where could she have gotten the bomb?"

"From the prop car, where I *put* it, after disassembling

181

it and storing it for evidence. That's more elmination. Nobody but someone riding with us on the train could have gotten into the prop car, retrieved the makings, and wired them back together. Anyone could figure out how the fool thing worked, but, lucky for Madame Sarah, Claudette set it an hour too early."

One of the Secret Service men whistled and said he'd see that Claudette was arrested in Frisco, and this time Jarret didn't argue. So Longarm shook all around and they parted friendly as he left to board his own train.

By the time he got back to Denver, Longarm had met up with a right friendly schoolmarm who couldn't get off there but said she'd never forget him. The *Post* on the newsstand in the Union Depot carried the story of Claudette Laval's arrest and full confession in Frisco. Madame Sarah had brought down the house on Market Street after replacing her murderous soubrette on short notice. When and if she got back east, she was invited to the White House. For Lemonade Lucy Hayes had decided that any gal who saluted the flag regular, got escorted to Christian worship by the Bishop of San Francisco, and had the whole damned country rooting for her, was likely good enough for her.

It was too early when they dropped him off in Denver for Longarm to get away with taking the rest of the day off. So he went on up to the federal building to see if Billy Vail had any afternoon chores in mind for him.

Vail greeted him friendly, for Vail, and shut the door after them as he led Longarm into his private office and waved him to a seat.

Vail got behind his own desk and said, "I just got a 'well-done' from Washington. For once you didn't screw up. There's hope for you yet, old son. When Mon-Sewer Sardou and his nasty sweetheart get out of *our* prisons, after serving time for criminal conspiring, the Republic of France wants to try 'em both for endangering their national treasure whilst packing French passports."

Longarm lit a cheroot with a match and a frown before he said, "That's letting Sardou off too easy, Billy. The son of a bitch didn't just conspire. He caused the spilling of *blood,* damn it!"

Vail leaned back and tented his fingers as he shook his head. "Let's not get technical, Longarm. Most of the blood was spilt by you, and I can't spare you. I know Miss Penelope Wayne was innocent and the Dorado Kid wasn't as mean as some thought. But you have to learn to pay attention. I told you that evil pair would do long stretches in U. S. prisons and then get handed over to the French."

"Mebbe so, but will the French cut their heads off like they ought to?"

"Likely not. The sentence I understand they have in mind is life. And if you've ever seen the inside of a French jail, you'll know why cutting their heads off would be doing 'em both a favor. I don't know where the Frogs send wicked she-males, but Lifers go to Devil's Island to get et alive by mosquitos whilst trying to survive on bread and water. I imagine, in years to come, they'll both look back wistful on their twenty years or so as guests of Uncle Sam."

Longarm nodded and said, "That sounds fair. I can't come up with anything more spiteful. So I'll leave 'em to Future Justice. Do you have anything in particular for me to do this afternoon, boss? I'm sort of stiff from the long train ride back. I'd kind of like to lie down a spell."

Vail chuckled and asked, "Who with? Don't tell me you didn't meet nobody on the train from Sacramento, old son. I know for a fact you were traveling Pullman."

Longarm didn't answer as he studied the tip of his cheroot. Vail laughed and said, "Never mind. I don't care who you met on the train coming *back*. Let's get around to the orders I gave you regarding Madame Sarah and company."

"It's all in my report, Billy. I done as you asked. I met 'em up in Cheyenne and didn't let nobody kill 'em till the Secret Service got back on the job."

Vail nodded. "Yeah, I said you did *that* right. But I know you of old, Longarm. You wouldn't be so tired this early in the day if you hadn't been screwing like a mink whilst I wasn't looking."

Longarm looked innocent and said, "All right, I met me

a schoolmarm on the eastbound flier and we may have got a mite friendly—on my own time."

"Bullshit. You got circles under your eyes, and I noticed how you was walking when we met. No one mortal woman could have taken that much lead outten *your* pencil, Longarm. 'Fess up. Did you disobey my orders about that Madame Sarah? I noticed what she looks like in tights, for I reads the *Police Gazette,* and they say she likes boys, too."

Longarm shook his head. "I never, Billy. You told me not to mess with her and I never disobey a direct order."

Vail rolled his eyes heavenward and growled, "Now I know you're lying like hell! I'll bet you *did,* you horny rascal! And if I hear anything about it, from either Washington or Paris, you're in one hell of a mess, hear?"

Longarm started to giggle. So naturally Vail asked him what in hell was so funny. "I don't care if you believe me or not. But I can give you my word on Bibles and salt that I never messed with Madame Sarah Bernhardt, serious."

Vail stared hard for a minute. Then he said, "Forget the Bibles and salt. Do I have your word as a *man* that you left the national treasure of France pure, Longarm?"

"Well, I can't say how pure she might or might not be. But I give you my word as a man she's still as pure as I found her."

Vail heaved a sigh of relief. "Hot damn. This is all too good to be true! Do I realize this is the first case I've sent you on, recent, that you failed to mess up? I was afraid you'd wind up in bed with the Divine Sarah, knowing both your natures. But since you swear you never, I have to believe you. Now you'd best go eat so's you can deliver a prisoner to court this afternoon."

Longarm swore softly and got up to go before Vail could ask him any more personal questions. He was grinning by the time he was out in the corridor and off the hook. Old Billy hadn't asked if he'd trifled with any other gal in Sarah Bernhardt's troupe. So he hadn't had to explain why save for the Divine Sarah, herself, he'd laid every damned one of 'em.

184

Watch for

LONGARM AND THE OUTLAW LAWMAN

fifty-sixth in the bold
LONGARM series from Jove

coming in June!